a STAR ON THE HOLLYWOOD WALK OF FAME

ALSO BY BRENDA WOODS:

My Name Is Sally Little Song
Emako Blue
The Red Rose Box

A STAR ON THE HOLLYWOOD WALK OF FAME

BRENDA WOODS

G. P. Putnam's Sons ★ An Imprint of Penguin Group (USA) Inc.

ACKNOWLEDGMENTS

Many thanks to John Rudolph for his careful attention to this manuscript and to my agent, Barbara, for her support. To everyone at Penguin Young Readers Group and to librarians and teachers who have supported me, thank you. As always, I honor the Spirit. Kindness is free.

G. P. PUTNAM'S SONS
A division of Penguin Young Readers Group. Published by The Penguin Group.
Penguin Group (USA) Inc., 375 Hudson Street, New York, NY 10014, U.S.A.
Penguin Group (Canada), 90 Eglinton Avenue East, Suite 700, Toronto, Ontario M4P 2Y3,
Canada (a division of Pearson Penguin Canada Inc.).
Penguin Books Ltd, 80 Strand, London WC2R 0RL, England.
Penguin Ireland, 25 St. Stephen's Green, Dublin 2, Ireland (a division of Penguin Books Ltd.).
Penguin Group (Australia), 250 Camberwell Road, Camberwell, Victoria 3124, Australia
(a division of Pearson Australia Group Pty Ltd).
Penguin Books India Pvt Ltd, 11 Community Centre, Panchsheel Park,
New Delhi—110 017, India.
Penguin Group (NZ), 67 Apollo Drive, Rosedale, North Shore 0632, New Zealand
(a division of Pearson New Zealand Ltd).
Penguin Books (South Africa) (Pty) Ltd, 24 Sturdee Avenue, Rosebank,
Johannesburg 2196, South Africa.
Penguin Books Ltd, Registered Offices: 80 Strand, London WC2R 0RL, England.

Published simultaneously in Canada. Printed in the United States of America.
Design by Marikka Tamura. Text set in Adobe Garamond Pro.
Library of Congress Cataloging-in-Publication Data
Woods, Brenda (Brenda A.)
A star on the Hollywood Walk of Fame / Brenda Woods. p. cm.
Summary: Nine Los Angeles high school students use a creative writing class assignment
to shed light on their own lives. [1. High schools—Fiction. 2. Schools—Fiction.
3. Los Angeles (Calif.)—Fiction.]   I. Title.
PZ7.W86335St 2010   [Fic]—dc22   2009008750
ISBN 978-0-399-24683-8
1   3   5   7   9   10   8   6   4   2

To my mother, Maxine

To my brothers and sisters:
Art, Brett, Allysyn, Alicia, Bart, and Brian

To our newest grandchild, Dominic, a light

And to the many splendid young people I have met
or received letters from over the years,
I hope you find what you are looking for on these pages.

'CUZ I'M A STAR

"ASSIGNMENTS ON THE DESK BEFORE YOU SIT," SHE reminded them as they rumbled in. "You know the drill."

There were only nine students in her tenth-grade creative writing class: Dorian Green, Mary Holly, Sunday Waters, Carlos Baraza, Marlon Pope, Shante Harris, Gus Little, Ronni Castillo, and Jake Peterson. It was Ms. Hart's smallest class.

One by one, they handed in their essays. All except for Marlon. Again.

"You have your assignment today, Marlon?" she asked.

"No, Miz Hart. I'll have it for you t'morrow," he said matter-of-factly.

Ms. Hart stared up at his face. "It's due today. Why tomorrow?"

"'Cuz I'm a star." Marlon threw an imaginary basket-ball through a hoop. "Three points," he added, then bowed, gathering laughs and boos from the class.

"*Because* you're a star," she corrected.

He smirked. "Miz Hart, this is creative writin', right? So, I'm creative talkin'."

Snickers bounced around the room.

But Ms. Hart didn't let it go. "So, Marlon, *because* you play basketball and *because* you're a star, you think you don't have to turn in your assignments on time?"

He tipped his head to the side and smiled sweetly, turning on the charm. "It's hard sometimes, Miz Hart. I get home late after practice, even later after games. By then I'm tired and all I wanna do is sleep. Why you gotta stress? I said I'll have it t'morrow. I promise . . . chill."

"That ain't hardly fair, Miz Hart," Sunday blurted out. "I mean why should the rest of us have to hand in our homework on time and he doesn't just because he's good at puttin' a ball through a hoop?"

Carlos nodded in agreement. "And some of the rest of us have important things to do after school . . . like work."

"What? And B-ball ain't important? How y'all gonna be like that? Weren't for me this school wouldn't even have a name. I'm the reason we made it to State last year, and I'll be the reason we make it again this year. Y'all remember this when I turn pro. Marlon Pope. Big-timin' with the Los

Angeles Lakers. Don't none a y'all even think about askin' me for jack."

Sunday started up again. "That's what's wrong with a-tha-letes . . . always expectin' special treatment."

Dorian, class clown and instigator, jumped to his friend Marlon's defense. "Be quiet, Friday. You know *my boy's* a shining star."

"My name ain't Friday!"

"Settle down," Ms. Hart told them.

Mary rolled her eyes toward the ceiling. "This is so immature." She typically acted like school was a waste of her time.

Marlon snarled at Mary. "Snot-ass."

"Enough!" Ms. Hart commanded. She decided to change her tactics. "Any other stars in the room besides Marlon?"

The room quieted as they glanced around. Cautiously, Shante raised her hand.

"What you the star of?" Dorian asked snidely.

"Dude, why you wanna disrespect her like that?" Jake scolded from his seat in the back. He had six inches and thirty pounds on Dorian.

Dorian backed down. " 'Scuze me, Jaaa-ake."

Shante gave Jake a flirty look before returning her gaze to Ms. Hart. "I take dance," she said. "And I'm real good. So I'm a star for that."

"Thank you, Shante. Anyone else?" Ms. Hart asked.

Gus surprised her by chiming in. Getting Gus to talk

was a chore—one Ms. Hart had almost given up. "Most people are just regular," he said softly.

Ronni flipped her hair. Her long lashes were thickly coated with black mascara, her nails painted frosty royal blue, her glossy brown mane perfect as usual. "Stars are beautiful," she said.

Ms. Hart turned to the board, picked up a piece of chalk, and printed WHAT IS A STAR?

Dorian shook his head. "Oh, no, here we go."

"Stars are famous," Sunday replied.

Ms. Hart scribbled *famous* on the board.

Ronni repeated, "Stars are beautiful."

But before Ms. Hart had finished writing *beautiful,* Dorian disagreed. "Some ain't."

Carlos smiled. "Stars are rich."

Sunday spoke up. "Then Marlon ain't no star becuz he sure ain't rich."

"But I will be," Marlon said confidently.

"You could get hurt," Carlos warned.

"That's what doctors are for, dawg." Marlon had an answer for everything.

"Stars ride in limos," Shante added.

"Who would even want to be a star?" Mary offered. "They don't have any privacy, and everywhere they go the paparazzi have cameras in their faces. And when they make a mistake, it's all over the news and the tabloids."

"Speak for yourself," Shante quickly countered. "Put a

hundred cameras in my face and drop gazillions in my bank account so I can buy me a three-story house in the hills above Sunset with an elevator and one of those infinity pools. Oh, yeah, sign me up yes-ter-day."

Dorian stood up and did a twirl with his arms above his head like a ballerina. As expected, muffled laughter from some of his classmates followed.

Sunday blasted him. "Why you gotta be a hater, Dorian? Wait and see." She locked eyes with her best friend, Shante. "I bet she'll even have one of those stars on Hollywood B."

"Yeah, a star on the Hollywood Walk of Fame," Shante said dreamily.

A question flashed into Ms. Hart's mind and flew out of her mouth. "What if you could get a star on the Hollywood Walk of Fame for all kinds of things?"

"Like what?" Carlos asked.

"Whatever you're good at," Ms. Hart replied.

"What if you're not good at anything?" Gus asked.

"Everyone's good at something," she answered.

Mary yawned. "This is tedious."

"Maybe you'd like to be somewhere else, Mary?" Ms. Hart asked.

"Soon enough," she muttered.

Undaunted, Ms. Hart scribbled A STAR ON THE HOLLY-WOOD WALK OF FAME on the board. "Write it down. If you could get a star on the Hollywood Walk of Fame for anything that you're good at, for anything good that you've done or plan to do, what would it be for? Make it the last entry in your journals, which are due in two weeks, and that goes for everyone, including Marlon and any other stars in the room. You have two weeks, so I expect something marvelous."

"I expect something marvelous," Dorian mocked.

Ms. Hart raised an eyebrow. "I heard that, Dorian."

Shante grinned. "You know we love you, Miz Hart."

A smile curled around Ms. Hart's lips as she glanced at her lesson plan. "Okay, today I'd like to review dialogue punctuation. I've noticed that most of you are having trouble with that."

Groans filled the room.

Thirty minutes later the bell screamed.

"T minus zero . . . time to roll out," Dorian said and zoomed toward the door.

"Don't forget . . . 'A Star on the Hollywood Walk of Fame' in your journals in two weeks," Ms. Hart called out as the nine joined the herd of kids in the hall. "And here's the deal—everyone gets dropped half a grade when they turn in late assignments . . . everyone."

"All becuz of Marlon," someone bellyached.

At the end of the day, Ms. Hart grabbed her briefcase plus an armful of books and butted outside through the double doors. Warm Santa Ana winds had blown the air clean, and the late afternoon sky was a clear sheet of blue. As she drove, she rolled down the window and tipped her face toward the setting sun. That's what Los Angeles does, she thought. It lures you with this picture-perfect-postcard kind of thing.

Miles from her apartment, she hit gridlock. Gridlock is something Angelenos expect—like oceans being filled with salt water, it's just the way it is. But Ms. Hart wasn't used to it yet, and it frustrated her. So while she sat in traffic, her mind headed home to New York City. She daydreamed about fall walks in Central Park, crunching through red and yellow fallen leaves, soccer balls tossed high by kids on the playing fields. She imagined a single kite sailing the sky and could almost hear the sounds of bongo drums and distant music.

It had been almost two years since she'd gotten her master's in creative writing at NYU and taken the teaching job at Fairfield High in Los Angeles instead of the one they'd offered in NYC. "You're making a big mistake, Zena," everyone had warned. Even her brother Carter had tried to convince her that Los Angeles was a wasteland populated by skinny, mindless, sunglass-wearing mutants. The City of Lost Angels, he'd called it.

"Warm winters, no snow," she'd simply replied.

Fairfield had offered her a contract for next year, and she pictured it on the kitchen table, where it had been sitting for weeks. Half of her wanted to stay, while the other half wanted to head back to NYC. Ms. Hart sighed, and turned on the radio.

By the time she got home, it was dusk. Her calico cat, Purple, crept along the kitchen counter while she sorted through the day's mail. The unsigned contract begged for attention, but instead Ms. Hart stared at the caricature her brother had drawn of her being pulled by a lasso to the City of Lost Angels. Holding it to the refrigerator door was an I ♥ New York magnet.

PUT THE BALL THROUGH THE NET, BABY BROTHER

(MARLON)

"SCOUTS FROM UCLA BEEN AT EVERY PRACTICE this week," I told Dorian as we ate lunch.

"Coolicious," he replied before stuffing a huge piece of lasagna in his mouth. The cafeteria was full of people and noise. On Tuesdays they always served some kind of Italian food. "You still turnin' pro after freshman year?" he mumbled.

"Hell, yeah. What kinda fool do I look like?"

Dorian grinned and shoveled another big bite in his mouth.

"Damn, don't your mama feed you?" I asked, expecting a comeback. But Dorian simply turned away and kept eating. Oh, well.

I took a sip of soda and gave a nod to one of my lovelies who'd come in with her girls. I was about to get up and go nibble on her ear or something when Carlos walked over with his tray. Before he could sit down, I let him have it. "Some of us have important things to do after school," I mocked. "And I thought we were cool. Get out my face!"

Carlos glanced at Dorian, looking for a defense. Dorian shrugged. "I think you in the doghouse."

"Sorry, Marlon," Carlos muttered before heading to another table.

I picked at the lasagna with my fork.

"Your food's 'bout to get cold, baby brother. Eat up," Dorian said.

"Listen up, dawg, don't ever call me that." I pushed away my plate.

Dorian stopped eating. "Baby brother? Why not?"

"Just don't!" I sprang to my feet, snatched my pack, and went to the gym.

Lucky for me it was deserted. I grabbed a ball from the bin, dribbled, and shot from the three-point line. As the ball sank through the net, Carlos's words from class rang through my mind: "You could get hurt." Then I couldn't play ball, which would most definitely make my big brother, Chris, happy. He's a sophomore at Yale. In fact, this whole basketball thing started with him, four years ago.

Our pops had nailed a hoop to the garage and created a half court in the backyard. We used to play after school, and every day Chris would taunt me as I stood at the free throw line. Like it was supposed to be easy.

Back then everything seemed easy for Chris. He was sixteen, buff, too smart, and thought he was all that. His smile was perfect and he had super-fine Queen Bees all over him. Your typical older brother asshole. Meanwhile, I was eleven, scrawny, and clumsy, with teeth that badly needed braces.

"Put the ball through the net, baby brother!" he shouted one afternoon.

I'll make it this time, I thought. *Then he'll shut his big trap.* I shot and missed. Total air ball.

Chris laughed as he retrieved the bouncing ball. From the edge of the yard, he sank a three-pointer. The ball rolled back to him and he scooped it up. "Come and get it, baby brother," he said, holding the ball over his head.

I hurtled toward him, but the concrete was uneven and the toe of one shoe caught the edge. I tripped and fell hard. Both of my knees were bleeding and burning. My ankle was twisted.

"Clumsy ass." Chris grinned. He sank another three-pointer and repeated, "Put the ball through the net, baby brother. It's easy."

Someday, I'll kill you, I thought as I limped into the house.

Chris had whupped me before. In fact, he was always whupping me, but all of a sudden I couldn't take it anymore.

"Put the ball through the net, baby brother," I mocked

as I watched him from the kitchen window, dribbling and dunking. Then I added, "I can . . . I will."

That was the day I became focused and single-minded, like one of those Buddhist monks. "I can . . . I will" was my mantra.

For the next few months I practiced secretly when no one was home, repeating "I can . . . I will" with each shot. Until one day, I made two baskets in a row, then three, then five, then a three-pointer.

I stopped playing computer games and began studying footage of basketball games. I forgot all about my boyz. "Why you don't hang with us no more?" they asked.

That summer I got lucky and grew six inches. Though only twelve, I was as tall as Chris, six-one. I started pumping iron, and by the end of the summer I began to get thick. Baby brother, hah!

Now that I had a few muscles and wasn't clumsy anymore, I easily made the middle school team.

"You have major skills, Marlon," the coach told me at tryouts.

"I can, I did," I told myself.

By eighth grade, I had shot up to six-five and even though I now had braces, beautiful young ladies of every color started hanging on me like designer clothes in a closet. Chris had gone away to college and I felt too good.

High school ball was even better. There were stories about me in the *Los Angeles Times* sports section that Moms got framed. Even when I was a freshman, colleges were already sending letters to my coach, scouting me during games, waiting in line to shake my hand and slip me their cards. I could spot them in the crowd. I got totally puffed up, feeling like I was finally out of Chris's shadow, higher than the moon, brighter than the sun.

"Marlon!" the crowds would scream from the bleachers when I stood at the free throw line. "Put it in, Pope!" they yelled.

They'd rise to their feet when I made a three-pointer.

"I can . . . I will," I said before each shot.

Then last summer when he was home on break, Chris, like an idiot, challenged me to a game of one-on-one. What a joke. Every time I got the ball, I sent it through the net with ease, laughing at his candy-ass attempts to block me. And when he tried to make a shot, I mimicked him, "Put the ball through the net, big brother. It's easy." At one point he missed seven in a row.

"Bow down," I told him when he'd finally had enough.

Chris gave me the finger. "Grow up," he said. "They've got ten thousand exactly like you thinking the NBA has jerseys waiting for them with their names on them. Instead of the NBA, you should be thinking about an MBA." He retreated into the house.

"Hater!" I yelled after him. *Damn*, I thought, *I whupped him. I did it.*

• • •

I glanced at the clock in the gym. Lunch period was almost over. I dribbled the ball back to the top of the circle and pictured myself with a fly shorty, a fantabulous crib, shoes that bore my name, and an entourage. I am Marlon Pope, star forward, the three-point man, destined for greatness and the Hall of Fame.

The bell rang as I shot the ball. It sank through the net.

"Three-pointer!" someone yelled from the doorway. It was Dorian.

I left the ball in the middle of the gym and met him at the door.

"You still mad?" he asked.

"Naw," I replied. "You comin' to the Truman game?"

Dorian grinned. "And miss *my boy* make history? That's a question you don't even have to ask."

Miz FiFi

(Shante)

"This better work," I told Sunday as we boarded the underground Metro Line after school. We were headed clear to East LA.

"You wanna stay cursed?" she asked.

"Would I be doing this if I did?"

"You bring the money?"

"Of course," I replied.

According to Sunday's cousin, Danielle, someone must have put *something* on me. Ever since the eighth grade, every boy I'd had a crush on had moved far away fast. And for the past six months, not even one had asked for my number. Some brother would make his approach, start a little conversation, and then back off like I had some kind of disease. I guess I did—a serious case of bad luck with the fellas. So when Sunday's cousin promised that this Jamaican psychic lady could change my luck for fifteen dollars, I figured it couldn't hurt.

Sunday pulled a book from her backpack and quickly immersed herself in it.

"Remember Lonnie Dash?" I asked, nudging her shoulder.

"Yeah, I remember him," she said as she continued to read.

"He was fine, huh?"

Sunday looked up from her book. "Shante, I gotta finish readin' this for history class by t'morrow and I'm only on page ten, okay?"

I shut up and let her read. And as the Metro zoomed, I remembered when the bad luck landed.

Lonnie Dash's skin was smooth and dark like chocolate. We were both in the eighth grade, and I thought he was way too fine. So did most of the other girls. Almost every week he was hugged up with a different one, whispering in her ear. He could have his pick, so the day he walked me to a table and sat across from me, I felt like I was really something. "Holler at you tonight," he promised after he asked for my number.

For five days straight, Lonnie Dash called me every night. But the very next week he moved to Orlando, where his pops had gotten a job at Disney World. Just my luck.

During summer vacation, I turned fourteen and bad

luck found me again. This time his name was Danté Beach. We met at the Laundromat where Mama had dropped me off because our washing machine at home was broken and dirty clothes were piling up fast. I was loading the washers when I turned and faced the prettiest pair of brown eyes I'd ever seen. *Too cute*, I thought. He was probably fifteen, maybe sixteen, and almost six feet tall. His skin was medium brown, hair cut close. He had a goatee and mustache. Staring into his eyes, it seemed like we were the only two people alive on Earth. Shante and Danté—love in an instant.

And that was how we came to be. Until the end of the summer, that is, when his mother got transferred to Oakland.

After Danté left, Sunday tried to comfort me. "I feel too sorry for you, girlfriend," she told me. "Maybe you're cursed?"

I didn't argue.

Many months later Harrison Hope walked into our classroom and immediately stole my heart. He had recently moved to LA from Hawaii because his father worked for this big computer company and got transferred a lot. Definitely cursed, I thought. But he told me his mother made his dad swear that they wouldn't move again for at least two years. I hoped Mr. Hope kept his promises.

The rest of freshman year was like heaven. Weekend meetings at the mall, Disneyland, Rollerblading at Venice Beach, more e-mails than you can count, text messages, sweet kisses at the top of the Ferris wheel on the Santa Monica Pier, hand holding.

Then his parents separated. Harrison headed back to Hawaii and I lost it—all hope, that is.

"Shante?" Sunday said loudly, startling me out of my daydream. "Hurry up. This is where we get off."

The house didn't have any address numbers, and the yard was wild with plants and trees. It looked vacant.

"You sure this is it?" I asked.

Sunday checked the address on the curb. "Has to be." We knocked on the door, and this old gray-haired woman answered. She had one brown eye, one green eye, and two gold teeth.

"Miz FiFi?" we asked.

"Come in, ladies," she replied. Cautiously, we entered.

Cobwebs were everywhere and curtains made from crystal beads hung in front of windows that were so dirty there was hardly any light in the rooms. All of the furniture was pink, the sofa, tables, lamps, everything. A live rooster was walking on the dining room table. Two black cats without tails and a dog with three legs were roaming around.

"This is creepy," I whispered to Sunday.

Sunday nodded and glanced toward the door like she was preparing to bolt. If she did, I planned to be right behind her.

Miz FiFi cackled. "You got my money?"

I leaned close to Sunday. "Her money?" I said in a low voice. "She didn't even do anything yet."

Miz FiFi must have heard me because her eyes started rolling around. "You don't want to pay me, but you got a ton a bad luck, don't you, girl?" she fussed.

"Only with the fellas," I explained.

"And you wanna continue along the bad luck trail or not?"

"Or not."

"And you think fifteen dollars is a lot to pay to be free of bad luck or not?"

"Or not," I repeated, handing her the money.

Miz FiFi ordered me to sit in a chair and lit some kind of dried leaves with a match. As smoke filled the dim room, she began chanting words that I couldn't understand.

"What's that you're burning?" I asked.

"Do not speak," the island lady warned.

"Sorry." My hands began shaking from nerves.

More foreign-sounding words and waving of arms followed. Then the rooster crowed twice and Miz FiFi proclaimed, "You are cured. Go and be quick! Before the spirit finds you and lands on you again."

Sunday and I sprinted from the house without looking back. We were half a block away when we heard the rooster crow again, followed by the old lady's laughter.

"I am never going there again," I said, panting.

Sunday's eyes were wide as she agreed, "Me neither."

It was almost four thirty and my dance class near downtown started at five. "See you tomorrow," I said as we rushed to different trains.

"Later," Sunday replied.

Four minutes before five I got off the Metro right across the street from the school and hurried, knowing my teacher, Madame Mink, would fuss if I showed up late. One foot was through the door when I saw Jake from Ms. Hart's class in the hallway.

"Hey, Shante," he said.

"Hey, Jake," I replied. "What are you doing here?"

"I started a music composition class today. It let out a few minutes ago."

"Oh, you write music?"

"I'm learning."

We gazed into each other's eyes, and suddenly nothing else mattered.

Madame Mink stepped into the hall. "Class will begin in two minutes. The door will be locked," she warned in her authoritative way.

"Gotta go," I told him.

That was when he spoke the magic words. "Maybe I could call you . . . we could talk? You good with that?"

I actually wasn't too surprised. Over the past few weeks,

I've caught him checking me out during English class. But wow, Miz FiFi's cure sure did work fast.

"Okay," I replied. I scribbled my cell number on a slip of paper and handed it to him.

He stared at it like I'd given him a winning lotto ticket and slipped it in his pocket. "I'll call you tonight."

Madame Mink was at the door, key in hand. I took one last look into his angelic eyes and scurried inside. From the other side of the glass partition he watched as we stretched and practiced, but after about fifteen minutes he left.

At first, I felt really happy because Jake is way too cool. But as class went on, I began to worry, partly about the curse but mainly because Jake is white. I've never really liked a white boy before, and to tell you the truth, I don't think most of them are cute. But Jake is, in that Justin Timberlake kind of way. Still, this wasn't quite what I had in mind when I went to Miz FiFi's.

I thought about Sunday. She and I have talked about the interracial thing before, and I know how she feels—not good. I decided not to tell her anything, yet. And when Mama picked me up from dance class, I wondered, *What will my parents think?* I'm not too worried about my mother, but I know Daddy won't like it.

That night, I had the room all to myself for a change. My older sister, Hayley, a.k.a. the Queen Bee, wasn't home yet. The clock in my room read ten fifteen. I checked my cell again. Still nothing. I slumped into my beanbag chair and waited.

Finally my cell rang. " 'Bout time," I blurted out.

Jake laughed. "We should do something . . . like meet at the mall."

"When?" I asked.

"Saturday?"

"I'll havta ask my parents," I told him.

Over an hour later, when we got off the phone, I felt higher than a kite. Instinctively, I punched in Sunday's number but quickly hung up. I knew for certain she would trip big-time, and I wasn't in the mood.

What I was in the mood for was sweet Jake Peterson.

I HOPE MAMA'S HOME

(SUNDAY)

BY THE TIME I GOT BACK FROM EAST LA, THE STREETLIGHTS were on.

Please let Mama be home, I thought. I really didn't like being alone with her latest, Mr. Sam Johnson.

The first time I met him, I warned her that he was going to be like all the rest. Mama smiled and said, "He's got a good job, Sunday, at City Hall. He even goes to church." And before I knew it, he was moved in and comfortable, with his feet propped up, a beer in one hand, the remote in the other.

But today on the long ride home I thought maybe this time I'm wrong. I wondered if I should give him a break like Mama keeps saying. I mean, he does slip me a twenty every two weeks when he gets paid, and he brings Mama a dozen red roses every Friday night. Plus Mama seems happy and he even bought her an engagement ring, a real one-carat diamond, she tells everybody. Mama asked me to call him Daddy after they get married. I don't really want to, but because my real daddy only seems to care about his new wife and kids, I promised her I would. I tried hard to convince myself that Mama had finally found a real husband-material brother.

That night, after we finished dinner, I cleared the table, trying to make a good impression, hoping Mr. Sam Johnson would really marry Mama and that he'd be the last. I did have on shorts, but it's not like they were Daisy Dukes or anything, just regular. But as I left the table, I noticed that instead of keeping his eyes on Mama, who was sitting across from him, his eyes stayed glued on me. You know, the way a young player watches because he wants to get with you . . . that way.

He'd looked at me like that a couple of times before but usually after he'd had more than a few beers. This was the first time he'd done it right in front of Mama.

Mama glanced at me, then at him. "Save those dishes for later, Sunday. Don't you have some schoolwork?"

"Done it already," I replied. Her eyes had lost that light of happiness.

"Then go to your room," she commanded.

I stormed to my bedroom and shut the door, but I could still hear them talking.

Mr. Johnson tried to defend himself. "You're imaginin' things, baby."

"Imagining?"

"You're tired, girl," he said sweetly. "Sit down and lemme give you a foot massage. You work too hard."

I turned on my portable fan, then squeezed a pillow around my head, muffling their words. They were still talking when I finally fell asleep.

"I could go live with Granny," I told Mama the next morning after Mr. Johnson had left for work.

"Why?" Mama asked, acting like nothing had happened as she barreled out the door on her way to her own job.

I yelled out, "Bye!" as the elevator doors swallowed her.

"What's wrong with you?" Shante asked when I saw her between classes. "Did someone die or something?"

"No."

"Then why do you look so morose? That's a word I learned yesterday. It means sad, if you didn't know."

"I know what *morose* means, moron."

"Moron? You must want a butt kickin', Sunday Waters."

I laughed loudly and tried to put Mr. Sam Johnson out of my mind. "So, are you still cursed?" I asked.

Shante gave me a funny look and said, "Later," before ducking into her class.

Instantly, my intuition told me, *Something is up with Miz Shante.*

So at lunch I asked again, "Did the Miz FiFi thing work yet?"

"Would you relax? It hasn't even been twenty-four hours," she replied. But the shifty look in her eyes told me she was hiding something.

"Whatever," I said and decided to let it go, because one thing I knew about Shante was she never kept the truth locked up for long.

That afternoon, when I got home from school, a neighbor lady who was going to get her mail told me the elevator was out of order. "Again."

"For real," I groaned and headed to the stairs. The elevator in our building was almost never working.

From outside our apartment I heard Mama's voice, singing along to her old-school music. I took a deep breath and put my key in the lock.

Two dozen red roses sat on the dining room table. Mama turned away from the stove where she was cooking dinner and grinned. "Hi, baby."

"Hey," I replied. She always called me baby when she was really happy.

Mr. Johnson was sitting in front of the television, watching basketball. "How 'bout these Lakers, Miss Sunday?" he asked without looking up. For a change, his hand was minus a beer bottle.

"Dinner'll be ready soon," Mama said, then started humming.

"I stopped and had a burger," I told her as I headed to my room and quietly closed the door. I sat on my bed and stared out the window. The little voice inside my head whispered, *You worry too much.*

Like Chrome in the Sun

(Carlos)

It was after nine o'clock when I finally dragged in from work.

"*Mijo?*" my mother called from her room.

"*Qué?*" I answered.

She spoke rapidly in Spanish, explaining that she was very tired and that dinner was on the stove. Leave enough for your father, she reminded me. My father, the hardest-working, least-tired man in the world.

"*Gracias,*" I said.

As I was loading my plate, I remembered I still had homework to do. I cursed under my breath in Spanish.

Go to school.

Go to work.

Go to sleep.

That's my life, working five days a week at the Half

Moon Bar and Grill, washing dishes. To be lazy? I never get the chance.

My father's words speak to me day and night. "We have to buy a house, Carlos . . . a house in America." It's my father's dream and so we work hard and save our money. "Even pennies become dollars," he says.

I was almost four years old when my parents and I came here from Guatemala, illegally. Some people don't even know where Guatemala is. They think that it's part of Mexico. "Is that near Cancún?" they ask. I get tired of explaining.

Though I read and write English well, some words are still hard because my parents speak mostly Spanish and it was the first language I learned. Spanish for me is like a pair of comfortable old shoes, but English feels different, like new shoes with the laces pulled too tight.

I flopped on the living room sofa that doubles as my bed and started my math. Then I thought about Ms. Hart's latest assignment, "A Star on the Hollywood Walk of Fame." Maybe I could get a star for being the most-tired fifteen-year-old alive or for worrying all the time about immigration. I keep hearing nightmare stories about raids and people being taken to detention centers. Luckily, it hasn't happened to anyone I know. Some people say they should send all of us who are undocumented home, but for the past eleven years Los Angeles has been the only home I know. Besides, my brother, Julian, was born here. What would happen to him? I keep telling my father to at least try to get a green card. So far, he hasn't.

My mind started to feel empty. As my head began to nod, the pencil dropped from my hand and my eyes closed.

It's moving day, and my father stands beside a U-Haul truck. My mother is next to him smiling, Julian under her wing like a baby chick. I snap a picture with one of those disposable cameras. This is a special day, and my mother always buys one for special days. The house we have traveled so far from home to obtain, the dream, is finally ours. We are gleaming from head to toe like chrome in the sun.

We load box after box of this and that, plastic flowers and vases, religious statues and candles with pictures of Jesus and Mary and the saints, refrigerator magnets, things that mean everything to my mother.

My father pats my back. "See, my son? It is worth it. America."

Soon the last box is loaded. I glance up at the window of the third-story one-bedroom apartment we have called home for the past eleven years and climb into the cabin of the truck.

The drive to the new development in Lancaster is a long one. Finally, we turn into a place where rows and rows of houses sit close together on small square patches of land, some with lawns of dirt. My father pulls into a driveway. The house is painted yellow with white trim. The new lawn is very green. I can't wait to see inside.

My mother points her face to the blue sky as we walk around the outside of our American dream. It's summertime, and the heat blazes. "Like Guatemala," she whispers.

I inspect the kitchen, new refrigerator, built-in microwave oven, and stove, running my hands along the tiled counter.

"Two bathrooms!" Julian calls loudly from upstairs.

"My room, which one?" I ask my father.

I follow his arm and dash upstairs to my room. It's small, but I don't care because it's mine. I sit down and touch the new carpet.

"Can I paint my room green?" Julian asks from his room across the hall.

"Later," my father replies. "First we unload."

Once we finish, we sit down to eat outside on the patio, gobbling Kentucky Fried Chicken from paper plates, gulping icy-cold Pepsi. Thousands of stars have filled the sky. When our stomachs are full, we load the garbage into our new trash cans.

That night I lie awake in my bed. My new bed.

"Carlos?"

The dream vanished, and I opened my eyes. My father was standing in the kitchen. My math book was still in my lap.

"Huh?" I mumbled.

"Your homework, it's finished?" he asked in Spanish, eating potatoes and meat straight from the pots my mother had left on the stove.

I squinted at the clock. It was almost eleven, still early in my father's eyes.

"Almost," I answered, picking up the pencil that had fallen to the floor.

He searched the refrigerator for a cold Corona. He popped it open and sat down wearily on the couch. "Today, *mijo*," he said, "today, I bought us a house."

"*Qué?*" I asked and wondered—am I still dreaming?

"I bought us a house," he repeated.

"In Lancaster?"

His eyes got big, round, surprised. "How did you know?"

I wanted to tell him that tonight I'd dreamed it, but instead I said, "I guessed because it's what you always talk about."

My father sipped his beer and sighed. "It's what we came here for. To America."

"I know," I replied, beaming.

"It's not built yet, but it will be finished by the summer. You and Julian will have to change schools," he said apologetically.

"That's okay. Does Mama know?"

"She will in a minute. There are papers to be signed."

"And I'll finally have my own room, right?"

"Yes, Julian too."

And Mama will make me take photos while we load the U-Haul truck, I thought, and we'll be so happy we'll be gleaming like chrome in the sun.

ONE WORD DAY

THE ENTIRE MORNING WAS TAKEN UP BY A STUDENT body assembly with a guest speaker, so every period was squeezed into a twenty-minute afternoon slot. By the time everyone sat down and roll was called, the bell was almost ready to ring again.

Most teachers hated these days, but for Ms. Hart, they were special—One Word Days. The students knew the game. No dictionaries allowed. Try to come up with the correct meaning of the word she had written on the board. After five minutes, everyone was asked to read their definition. Then she would tell them the real meaning. Anyone who was right got ten extra credit points.

Ms. Hart scrawled the word *scintillate* on the board.

Carlos scratched his head. "How do you say it?" he asked.

"Sin-til-ate," Ms. Hart replied.

"Why you always gotta pick words most folks ain't never heard before?" Dorian asked.

"That's how we learn new things," she replied.

Dorian kept the ball rolling. "What if we don't wanna learn new things?"

She sighed and shook her head, wishing for the umpteenth time that Dorian would just go along with the program. "Five minutes," she told him and set the timer on her desk.

Five minutes later, the timer rang. "Who wants to be first?" She waited for someone to raise a hand.

No response.

"Okay, then we'll do it by seat, starting in the back of the class."

Groans and giggles.

"Jake?"

Jake stood up. He was so easygoing that she often called on him first. "It probably means something that isn't like everything else. Somethin' different. Like, you have ten of something and one is different from the rest, so it stands out. Yeah . . . it scintillates."

Shante smiled up at Jake like there was something going on between them.

Dorian noticed it too. "Check it out, y'all. Salt and Peppa lovebirds," he snickered.

Shante slapped his arm. "You need to grow up, Dorian."

"Settle down. We don't have much time," Ms. Hart reminded the class and continued. "Sunday?"

Sunday's puzzled eyes shifted from Shante to Jake before she answered. "I gotta admit it, Miz Hart. I don't have a clue."

"Marlon?"

"What up?"

"The word *scintillate*?" she asked impatiently.

"I wrote a poem for the answer."

Ms. Hart cocked her head. "In five minutes?"

"I got it like that. Can I read it?" he asked.

"Of course."

Marlon stood and read from a piece of notebook paper. "I am great. Because I scintillate. The way I shine. I leave everyone behind. A'ight?"

"Very nice, Marlon. . . . Ronni?"

Ronni looked up from filing her nails. "I dunno . . . something that's not on time?"

Ms. Hart forced a smile. "Mary?"

Mary was smart and she knew it, which made her all the more infuriating. "It means something that twinkles like stars."

Marlon mocked her in a girl-like voice, "It means something that twinkles like stars."

Mary twisted her face angrily at him and mouthed what Ms. Hart thought were the words "I hate you."

"Hey, what is with you two?" Ronni asked Mary.

Mary clenched her teeth.

For once, Ms. Hart was glad when Dorian piped up. "Scintillate? This about that 'Star on the Walk of Fame' thing, huh?"

She couldn't help but laugh out loud. "You're right. *Scintillate* . . . to sparkle or twinkle . . . to be clever or witty." Right then, the bell rang, signaling the end of class. "Okay, game over. Pass in your papers. Everyone with the right definition will get ten extra credit points. And don't forget your journals and the 'Star on the Hollywood Walk of Fame' entries. I expect something that scintillates."

Candy-Apple Red

(Ronni)

My printer was spitting out a new batch of **Makeovers by Ronni** business cards when I noticed that the blue polish on my nails was already chipping. Time for a change. I scanned my endless collection of colors and picked a glittery black. But when I plopped on my bed to do my nails, my algebra book dropped on the floor and fell open to where I'd stuck my latest test. Another D.

I shook my head. If my dad hadn't promised me his old Honda Prelude in exchange for at least a C in algebra, I never would have taken that class. The counselor had warned me that I'd have to study hard. Me, study hard? What a joke.

Of course, exactly at that moment, my dad passed by my room and asked, "Do you have homework, Veronica?"

"No!" I lied. "And you're the only person who still calls me Veronica. . . . Would you stoppit already?"

"If you want the car—"

"If I want the car, what?" I interrupted, knowing what he would say.

"You'll study."

You know what you can do with your little piece-of-crap car, I thought as I got up and slammed the door.

The car is a piece of crap, almost. It needs major work: brakes, tires, a new alternator, new fuel pump, detailing. But because my dad has waxed that car weekly, the one thing it doesn't need is a paint job. It's shiny candy-apple red. Beautiful. And I want it.

In fact, the reason I started **Makeovers by Ronni** was to get money to fix it, and I almost have enough saved. People are always willing to pay to look better. Lucky for me, it's the one thing I'm good at.

While I worked on my nails, I kept glancing at the math book. I have another test coming up next week, and every time the math teacher mentions after-school tutoring in the library, I swear she looks straight at me. Give me a break. No way am I walking through those doors. I'm much too fly for that.

But the big red D glared, and I wanted my own ride. There had to be a way.

I started thinking really hard about who I could get to

help me. Then Mary from Ms. Hart's class popped into my mind. She's super smart. Everyone knows that. She even tutors. And she's in desperate need of a makeover.

It was the perfect plan. I decided I'd ask her tomorrow after class. I pictured myself behind the wheel with the music bumping and giggled.

PRETTY GEORGIE

(JAKE)

I'D LOST MY KEYS AGAIN. "UNLOCK THE DOOR!" I YELLED.

My older brother, Cue, let me in. The trailer was hot as an oven. I left the door open.

"What do you think this is . . . a sauna?" He was still half asleep, so I got no reply. I opened the windows to let in more air.

Cue scratched the back of his neck, then rubbed the top of his shaved, round head—hence the nickname Cue Ball or Cue.

Cool air began to fill the narrow metal rectangle we call home. It's an old, long, silver trailer in a park that's butted up against a cemetery, which can get kind of creepy.

Cue plopped back down on the sofa, his exhausted eyes glued to the TV. His regular after-work routine. "Mom called. She's going to dinner and a movie with Ruby." Ruby's a friend of our mom's who used to take care of us when we were little. She always has at least five cats and, hot or cold, wears hand-knitted hats. "And some young lady called . . . said her name was Ashanti or Shanta . . . something like that."

"It's Shante," I corrected him. I decided to wait until after nine to call her back. Calls before that seemed lame, I thought as I headed to my super-tiny bedroom.

Immediately, I started daydreaming about Shante—her sweetness, those eyes, that perfect smile, the way she covers her mouth when she laughs. I remembered the day in Ms. Hart's class when she proclaimed herself a star. After watching her dance, I know she can do it. And Shante is more than pretty—she's beautiful. When Shante's around, I feel like I'm hang gliding through clouds.

As I sat down at my keyboard to play a few songs, it hit me. Dancing injects her with the same pure joy music gives me. I grinned and made a promise to write a song about her.

I finished off a bag of Doritos I'd been working on, did some history homework, and started the Hollywood Walk of Fame entry in my journal. But as soon as the clock struck nine, I dialed her number. At the sound of Shante's hello, I melted. She was guilty of robbery—a thief who'd stolen my heart.

We'd been talking for over an hour when she mentioned that she was thinking about taking acting classes.

"My mom was in a movie once," I boasted.

"For real?" Shante sounded excited.

"You probably never heard of it, one of those indie films . . . about five years ago."

"What was the name of it?"

"*Pink Butterflies.* And she was on TV lots of times, and she even went to the Cannes Film Festival once with this guy she used to date who was a producer."

"Cool," Shante replied. "What's her name so I can look her up on the Internet?"

"Georgie Peterson . . . that was her movie name. Her real name's Georgette, but when she was younger, most people called her Pretty . . . Pretty Georgie. Her wanting to be in the movies is how we wound up in LA."

"Where'd you come from?"

"Minnesota."

Like balls at a batting cage, Shante's questions kept coming. "So how long have you been in LA?"

"Since I was three."

"What's your mom done lately?"

"Nuthin'. She gave it up, and now she works for this insurance company."

Shante sounded disappointed. "How come?"

Should I tell her the whole story about how the producer had given my mom HIV? And how when he died, he'd left her only enough money in his will for her to buy this trailer and how she'd let Hollywood go because she needed a job that was more reliable with good insurance benefits? My inner voice said no. So instead I told her, "She just gave up."

"Well, I'm not giving up," Shante said confidently.

We talked a little more about school and stuff. Finally, I asked her what I'd wanted to ask all night. "You wanna hang out at the Grove on Saturday?" The Grove was the mall not too far from school. "Or we could go to the mall in Glendale, the Americana. You ever been there?"

"No, but I've been wanting to," she replied.

At eleven o'clock on the dot, we said good night. I was back at my keyboard composing, struggling with the melody for Shante's song, when Cue came in. "Dude, you hungry?" he asked.

I glanced up. "Yeah."

He picked up my journal, which was open on the bed. "'A Star on the Hollywood Walk of Fame.' What's that about?"

"How if we could get a star for anything what would it be for."

"Oh, I thought it was about Mom. Remember how she used to always say she was going to get a star on Hollywood Boulevard? How many times did we walk up and down both sides of that street, reading the names?"

"Too many."

"Jack in the Box sound good?"

"Yeah, a double bacon cheeseburger and fries," I replied.

Cue hesitated in the doorway like a stalled car. "Is she black?" he asked. "You know, Ashanti."

I corrected him again. "It's Shante. . . . Why do you care?"

"It's the name. I wondered."

"And a white girl can't be named Shante, right?"

"I never met one," Cue replied. "Well, is she?"

"Yeah."

"Does Mom know?"

"No, but why? Mom's cool. She taught us right. Color doesn't matter."

Cue rolled his eyes. "That's what parents say. But when it comes to dating and all that, it can be a completely different story."

"Mom's not like that."

"Whatever. But remember when I dated Alana Mendoza?"

"Yeah," I told him, even though I really didn't.

"And then I dated that Moroccan girl, Monique?"

Monique I remembered. She was too beautiful to forget.

"And then the Asian girl, Natasha?"

"The one who dragged you to art museums all the time?"

"Yeah, her. Anyway, one day Mom asks, 'Can't you find a white girl?'"

"You're lying."

"Nope," Cue replied.

I looked at my brother long enough to detect the truth in his eyes. "Like I care what she thinks," I grumbled.

"Dude, I'm not tellin' you to care—I don't. What I'm sayin' is the ebony-ivory thing might really set her off." Cue paused, then asked again, "Double bacon cheeseburger and fries?"

"Yeah," I replied. And as he screeched off in his beat-up bucket, I stared at my keyboard and shook my head. *Why do people waste their time caring about things that shouldn't matter, like the color of someone's skin?*

He Gave Me Butterflies

(Mary)

I was barely out of the classroom when Ronni tapped me on the shoulder.

"Hi, Mary."

Why was she even talking to me? She never had outside of Ms. Hart's class. I thought I didn't exist to girls like her. At least that's the way the popular-gorgeous ones always treat me.

"Can I help you?" I asked.

"That's what I was going to ask you," she said, tagging along beside me in the hall.

I gave her a dirty look. "Do I look like I need your help?"

Glamour girl pursed her lips like she was holding back the truth. "Um . . . well . . . I do these makeovers with before and after pics, and I wondered if you might be interested. You have a pretty face."

"I have a pretty face? Have you also noticed that I'm fat?"

"But you're losing weight," she said.

I am, but I didn't trust her.

"Is this a joke? Did Marlon put you up to this?"

"No, but what is it with you two, anyway? You act like two attack dogs."

So she didn't know the story. I thought everyone did. "Nothing," I lied.

Ronni gave me a sideways glance that said she hadn't swallowed the lie, then handed me a card. "Whatever. If you decide you want a makeover, give me a call or e-mail me. It's all there. Remember, it's all about hair and makeup." She riffled through her stuff. "And here, take this." It was the latest *InStyle* magazine. "It might give you some ideas. Later," she added with a finger wave as a swarm of kids parted for the beautiful one to make her way down the hall.

I stared at the card. **Makeovers by Ronni.** A pretty face? Me? No one but my mom and grandma had ever told me that. Why was Ronni being so nice to me? I unzipped my backpack, slipped the card and magazine inside, and rushed to my next class.

As soon as I got home from school, I hurried to the bathroom, where I weigh myself twice a day. One hundred seventy, the numbers glared back at me, the same as yesterday. I almost let that freak me out but decided not to. At least I hadn't gained. Plus, people like Ronni had begun to notice that I'm losing weight.

Before last year, when I added over seventy-five pounds to the hundred twenty I already had, I was just another geek girl. At school, I spent most of my free time in the library. Even at home, instead of being on the computer, I preferred to read. With my nose in a book, I felt happy. I was average size, very easy to ignore, and as plain as my name, Mary, until I added the weight and became Fat Mary. For the record, fat is so much worse than plain.

Gaining the weight was the second biggest mistake of my life. Last year, right before summer break, I made a bigger mistake—I developed a serious crush on Marlon Pope.

I'm not a genius or anything, but I'm pretty smart. So I tutor after school in the school library, and one day Marlon showed up. I taught him Spanish twice a week for almost a whole semester, and I felt really lucky because Marlon is not only a basketball star, he's extremely cute. Being near him gave me butterflies.

When he got a good grade on a test, which, thanks to my help, was pretty often, he would act like he sort of liked me, laughing and trying to make jokes. A few weeks before summer break, when he finally got an A, he hugged me. And for the next couple of days my head was swimming in deep crush ecstasy. That's when I made my fatal error.

Marlon and I were alone in the tutoring room and I was sitting beside him as he conjugated Spanish verbs on the computer, wishing that he would turn around and give me a delicious first kiss, when all of a sudden I blurted, "Maybe we could go to the movies or something?"

He smiled and I thought, That's okay, a smile is good. But his smile quickly disappeared and was replaced by a sneer that made me wish I could take my words and stuff them back into my mouth.

"Me . . . be seen . . . with you?" he asked loudly. "You gotta be kiddin'."

I tried hard to keep from crying, but I couldn't hold back the tears. So I snatched my backpack and ran, fast. By the time I got home, I'd come up with twenty-seven ways to end my life. But instead I headed straight for the refrigerator. I grabbed a full half gallon of double-chocolate-chip ice cream and each huge, sweet mouthful seemed to make me feel better.

When I'd finished the whole container, a weird kind of calm zone enveloped me, and Marlon's rejection didn't hurt quite so much. And that was the start of my second biggest mistake—stuffing myself morning, noon, and night.

Becoming Fat Mary took gallons of ice cream, hundreds of bags of chips, anything fried, doughnuts by the dozen, my stomach stretching bigger and bigger, aching with comfort.

When I tipped the scale at 195, my mom began waving her Bible and proclaimed me a glutton, calling me a sinner.

Enter the diet and weekly trips to the nutritionist.

After I got off the scale, I stretched out on my bed and flipped through the *InStyle* magazine Ronni had given me.

Why do I torture myself? I thought, thumbing through the pages. Are there really this many beautiful people out there, or is it all about hair and makeup like Ronni claims?

I stopped on a page with an ad of a skinny girl wearing a metallic bikini who looked like she wasn't much older than me. I made the inevitable comparisons: She's tall—I'm average. She has a perfect body—I never will, no matter what. Her hair is pure copper-colored shine—mine, a thick, dark-brown mass of wavy frizz.

I stared at the photo, wishing I could figure out some way to replace my narrow eyes with her enormous, green, catlike ones. "What does it feel like to be so beautiful?" I asked her.

Talking to a magazine photo? I waited for the girl in the picture to say something, but she didn't. Okay, so I'm not a nutcase yet.

"When you walk into one of those really expensive restaurants where they serve you tiny portions of food on big plates, do people stop talking or eating to watch you go by?" I imagined myself there, sitting at a really bad table near the kitchen.

"And do you vomit right after you eat, or do you wait until you get home? I tried that once—no fun at all. Plus I read this story about a bulimic girl whose teeth fell out and she wound up in the hospital, where they fed her through a tube. That's all I need, to be toothless, with a tube taped to my nose.

"Do you have all these guys who look like Marlon clones begging to take you to clubs where rich and famous movie stars and celebutantes hang out, cuddling their miniature pooches?

"I bet your friends secretly hate you because you're way too pretty and they're afraid you'll steal their boyfriends, right?

"I've never had a boyfriend, and I've never even been on a date. And after what happened with Marlon, I wonder if I ever will, because he told lots of people. So for the last few weeks of school before summer break, they mocked me and made fun of me every day. Since school started, most of his crew has quieted down—I suppose the summer gave them other things to think about. But the weight gain gave plenty of fuel to other assholes."

The cat-eyed girl in the photo was turning into my new best friend. She was listening to every word I said. I could start to like this.

"And now the only girls who want to hang out with me are the other lard asses.

"I know what you're thinking. . . . No one forced me to put the food in my mouth, so why am I bellyaching?

"Okay, so, yeah, you're right, but it doesn't give anyone the right to ridicule me daily, calling me Fatty and making pig noises under their breath.

"Secretly I hope they'll wake up with hideous zit-covered faces or, even better, leprosy. Then they would understand how it feels.

"Sometimes I think that if one more creep at school treats me like I'm vermin, I might go to plan B—drop out as soon as I'm sixteen, which is in four months, take the GED, and head to college. What do you think?"

I waited for an answer. Nothing.

"For right now, though, I'm trying to be proactive. That's the word the nutritionist lady uses. I'm trying my best to keep up this healthy diet she put me on, and so far in less than three months I've lost twenty-five pounds. I wish it would hurry up faster, but then I'll wind up with saggy skin everywhere, she says.

"I hate being fifteen. But I bet for you it wasn't so bad. I bet everything for you is better.

"I used to beg God to be beautiful like you," I confided to the girl. "But right now I'd give anything to be like I used to be. You know, normal size."

I took my long hair out of the ponytail I normally wear

it in and stared at myself in the mirror. Maybe Ronni's right. Maybe it's all about hair and makeup.

I glanced at the girl in the metallic bikini. "What do you think, should I let glamour girl make me over or not? I mean, what am I supposed to be, her crowning achievement? If she can make me look good, then anything is possible?

"Or do I really have a pretty face?"

INVISIBLE

(GUS)

HOPING NO ONE WOULD SEE ME AND CALL THE COPS, I quickly climbed into the apartment through the window. I pictured the police, with their sirens blaring, screeching to a halt outside my door, and had to laugh. Things like that never happen to people like me—a quiet, short kid with a hairless face. To most people, I'm invisible.

I made myself a promise to stop forgetting my keys, fixed a tuna sandwich, and turned on the TV.

"Hi, Gus," my mom said as she opened the front door.

"Hi," I replied.

"You eat?"

"Tuna."

"Oh," she said as she rummaged through today's mail.

"Anything for me?" I asked.

She gave me that "of course not, you're only fifteen" look and replied, "Bills and junk mail. How was school?"

"Fine."

"You do your homework?"

"Yeah," I lied.

"Gus?"

"Huh?"

"Homework?"

"It's not that serious. Only history, and I have to read some book for a book report." I turned up the volume on the TV.

"Have you even started the book?"

I rolled my eyes. "No, but you know I'm a fast reader."

"Turn it off," she commanded. "And do your homework. I don't want any surprises when your grades come."

I clicked off the television and headed to my room, mumbling under my breath.

"And don't give me attitude, young man," she shouted behind me.

"You need to chill," I told her and shut my door. I lay down on my bed, stared at the ceiling, and started to listen. In this paper-thin-walled, eight-unit building you can hear almost everything: toilets flushing, doors opening, arguments and loud folks laughing, babies crying and water running. I've been in almost every apartment because my uncle, who owns the building, doubles as the handyman and sometimes he brings me along to help. I really don't mind—he always slips me a little cash.

Above me I heard old Miz Rosenthal. Cane, left foot,

right foot, cane, left foot, right foot. She has a rhythm all her own.

I forgot about homework, and while Miz Rosenthal kept time with her cane, I shut my eyes and played my favorite game. *Invisible.*

My mind went to my most frequently visited place, upstairs to apartment number six, where Ronni Castillo lives. She's in some of my classes. My imagination was on overdrive as I tiptoed into Ronni's room. Why I tiptoed I don't know—after all, I was invisible.

There she was, Ronni-so-lovely, skin smooth and light caramel, golden brown eyes. As usual, she was wearing skin-tight jeans. Wow! I imagined her wearing a pink tank top. I liked her in pink. And her lip gloss was pink too, my favorite.

Her cell phone rang. "Hey, girl," she answered.

While she talked, I glanced around. Huge stuffed animals crowded her room: lions, teddy bears, cats, a red Elmo, Big Bird, Bert and Ernie, Winnie-the-Pooh. She has a laptop, a flat-screen TV, and this big four-poster bed with fluffy pillows.

"Gus is real cute," she said to her friend.

I loved this game. I had Ronni change to speakerphone, so I could hear both sides of the conversation.

"He is," her girl agreed. "But he's kinda short," she added.

"I don't care. He has that pretty black curly hair," Ronni

said. Oh, yes! She likes my hair. I ran my fingers through it and sighed. "But every time I see him he doesn't have much to say. He's even quiet in class."

"Shy?"

"Yeah," Ronni agreed.

"You gonna invite him to your party?" the other girl asked.

"Pro'bly."

I knew she was having a party because her mom had mentioned it to mine. So far, I hadn't gotten an invitation.

A loud thump from above brought me back to my room. I was visible again. The sound of breaking glass followed.

I listened for Miz Rosenthal's rhythm, cane, left foot, right foot. Silence.

"Mom!" I yelled. "Miz Rosenthal!"

"What?"

"I think she fell," I said, bolting toward the front door.

"Again?" she asked as I headed out the door to the stairs. She followed me upstairs.

When I got to the apartment, I knocked softly and called out, "Miz Rosenthal," but she didn't answer.

I tried to peek through her windows, but the curtains were pulled shut.

This time, I banged and yelled. I felt charged up like a high-volt battery, which was unusual for me. "Miz Rosenthal, you okay?" No reply. I tried the door. Locked.

I took control. "Call 911!" I ordered my mom, and she hurried back downstairs.

Carelessly, I ripped the screen off the window. Luckily, it was unlocked.

I found her crumpled on the floor of the living room, surrounded by broken glass from what had most likely been a vase. Her face looked pale. She'd already had a stroke, and the last time she'd fallen, she'd broken her hip. Her cane with four little prongs at the end was on the floor beside her. It didn't look like she was breathing.

For a second, the real Gus got scared that she was dead. But the supercharged me got it together and shook her shoulder. "Miz Rosenthal?" No response. I tried hard to remember all of my Boy Scout stuff. I turned her on her back and checked her breathing and pulse. Nothing.

Quickly, I cleared as much of the broken glass out of the way as I could, but small leftover pieces still cut into my knees as I started CPR. I tipped her chin up and breathed into her mouth twice like I'd been taught, then I pressed on her chest. But I'd forgotten how many times to push, and Miz Rosenthal was tiny. I hoped I wasn't being too rough.

I kept at it, listening for the ambulance, praying they would hurry up. "Mom!" I yelled. Where was she? I needed help. I glanced toward the door. No one.

Time felt like it was running away fast. I breathed into her mouth again, then pressed on her chest over and over.

Her dentures were loose, and I took them out. That should have messed with me, but for some reason it didn't.

Finally my mom showed up and took over the CPR, and seconds later, I heard sirens.

"C'mon, Miz Rosenthal, don't die," I whispered.

The paramedics put this bag thing into her mouth and started pumping it to help her breathe. Then they hooked her up to a heart monitor. There was nothing but a flat line. One of them grabbed two paddles and jolted her with electricity, like you see on medical shows. I watched her tiny body arch, but the line on the monitor was still flat. They tried it again. This time the machine started beeping.

I took a deep breath. "She gonna live?" I asked one of the paramedics.

"Hard to say," he answered.

"I did the best I could," I told them.

He patted my shoulder. "You did great, kid."

"She have any family?" another asked.

Mom answered, "I called her son. He lives in Pasadena, but he's on his way."

"We're taking her to Cedars Sinai Medical Center. You can let him know."

By the time they got Miz Rosenthal downstairs to load her into the ambulance, a small crowd had gathered. That was when I noticed her: Ronni.

"You okay, Gus?" she asked.

I nodded.

She stared at my knees. "You're bleeding."

Suddenly I felt a little taller. "It's nothing."

"Is she gonna die?" she asked.

"I hope not."

"Me too," Ronni said as the ambulance sped away, its siren blaring.

"Hi, Ronni," my mom interrupted.

"Hi, Mrs. Little," Ronni replied.

I looked at my mom as if to say please go away.

"Oh," she said and turned to go inside. "I'll look at your knees later."

"Yeah, later."

"Mija?" Mr. Castillo called out from the top of the stairwell.

"What?" Ronni answered.

"Come inside. It's late."

"In a minute. I'm talking to Gus."

I waved at him and he smiled at me, then headed back to their apartment.

"You know, Gus . . . I'm having a sweet sixteen party on Saturday," Ronni said.

I wanted to say I know.

"It's really late notice, but you're invited."

"Thanks," I replied.

"And you can bring someone, if you want. I'll put the

invite in your mailbox because you can't get in without it. Or if you give me your e-mail address, I can send you an Evite and you can print it on your computer."

"My printer's broken," I told her.

"Then I'll put it in the mailbox. Later, Gus," she added and headed upstairs.

"See ya, Ronni," I replied, grinning, hoping she wouldn't forget.

That night as I lay in bed, my mind was dizzy. I felt so good about helping old Miz Rosenthal, and being invited to Ronni's party was awesome. After a while, I got drowsy and yawned, but right before I fell asleep, I played the invisible game again. I headed straight to Ronni's room, but this time I brought a pint-sized Cupid with me. When we got there, I made him take out a golden arrow and aim it straight at Ronni's heart.

NOT DAISY DUKES

(SUNDAY)

SOME OF THE FELLAS TURNED AND STARED AT SHANTE AS SHE squeezed in beside me on the bleachers. With Shante it's like that. "I thought you had dance class?" I asked her.

"And miss this game? You gotta be kiddin'."

We were playing Truman, Fairfield's archrivals, the team who'd beaten us last year at State and gone on to the Nationals.

Shante seemed nervous as she scanned the crowd. I was about to ask her who she was looking for when Jake showed up. "Can you move over a little bit, Sunday?" she asked.

"For who?" I replied, staring up at Jake. He was grinning like a kid on Christmas morning.

"For Jake," Shante replied, trying to make room.

"Naw, girly, no way—that white boy and you? You ain't even about that!" I whispered.

"He's nice . . . plus you shouldn't be prejudiced."

"I'm not prejudiced, I'm smart," I told her as Jake slipped in beside her.

"Hey, Shante," he said, then added, "hey, Sunday."

"Yeah, hey," I replied with a roll of my eyes.

"Don't be mean," Shante mouthed.

"He only wants one thing, and you know what that is," I said under my breath. Shante put her finger to her lips as if to say shut up.

Jake interrupted, "Good turnout. Hope Marlon can do us proud."

"Whatever," I muttered as the cheerleaders started their routines.

"You ever think about being a cheerleader?" I heard Jake ask Shante. "With your dancing and all, you'd probably be good."

"I'm a serious dancer, ballet and jazz. It's not the same," she explained.

I put my hand to my mouth and faked a yawn.

"You need to stoppit," Shante commanded.

I ignored her and joined in with the cheering, stomping my feet, yelling at the top of my lungs. The guy on the loudspeaker introduced the players one by one, and when he got to Marlon, everyone on our side of the bleachers stood up and yelled, "Put it in, Pope!" over and over.

By the time the game started, the crowd was on fire, and Marlon delivered. He made so many three-pointers that by halftime, Fairfield was ahead by twenty points.

The sorry Truman cheerleaders took the floor, and I excused myself to go to the ladies' room. When I got back, I couldn't believe my eyes. Shante and Jake were holding hands.

How many times had she and I talked about how different white folks and black folks were? And now here she was, the best friend I'd ever had, hugged up with a white boy. *So this was the secret Shante was keeping.*

By the fourth quarter, I wished I was somewhere else. We now had a sixteen-point lead, and I figured we had the game in the bag, so I got up to leave.

"I'm finna bounce," I told them.

"But the game's not over," Jake told me.

I pointed up at the scoreboard, but suddenly the crowd got quiet. Marlon was on the floor, holding his knee, writhing in pain. The referees called a time-out, and our coaches rushed to his side. When he finally got up, his teammates had to carry him to the bleachers.

I thought about all the bragging he'd done about the NBA. "Maybe he won't be big-timin' with the Lakers, after all," I told Shante.

"It's probably nothing serious," she replied.

The Fairfield crowd gave Marlon a standing ovation, and the game resumed. Without the three-point man, there was no telling what could happen, so I decided to stay for the rest of the game. We won, but only by six points.

"You need a ride home? My mom's coming to pick me up," Shante offered when the game was over.

"Naw, it's only four blocks. Later."

"Bye, Sunday," they replied at the same time, the way couples do. I glared at them and split.

Gus was standing outside, looking like he was waiting for a ride. He was so shy in class that at first I wondered if he could talk. The way I figure, it's probably all the jokes about him being short and his last name being Little that has him beat down. The fellas call him Little Man, and the girls mostly ignore him. But probably because people sometimes make fun of my name being Sunday, I feel kind of sorry for him. "Hey, Gus," I said.

"Hi, Sunday," he replied so softly I could barely hear him. "Too bad about Marlon," he added.

I repeated Shante's words. "It's probably nothing serious. At least we won!"

Gus agreed. "Yeah, but I hope he'll be okay."

"He will be. See ya." As I walked away, my mind turned back to Jake and Shante. A blue-eyed white boy? I needed to have a serious conversation with *my girl*. I checked my cell to see if she had sent me a text yet. Nothing. So I sent her one: have u lost ur mind? call me later.

The moon was full, lighting the streets as I walked the four blocks home.

When I opened the door to our apartment, there he was, in front of the TV as always.

"Hi, Mr. Johnson," I said. "Mama home?"

"Had to work overtime," he replied. "Where you been so late, Miss Sunday?"

I headed to the kitchen. "Basketball game."

"Y'all win?" he asked, following me.

"Yeah, but only by six points because our star player got hurt," I replied as I rummaged through the refrigerator, looking for something to eat.

"You hungry? We could order a pizza."

"That's okay. I'll make a sandwich."

Suddenly he shut the refrigerator door and stood in front of it. He grabbed my arm.

"What's wrong, Mr. Johnson?"

"I like you, Sunday," he replied.

His breath smelled like alcohol. The look in his squinty brown eyes and the tightness of his grip on my arm spelled big trouble.

Be smart, Sunday, I thought. I smiled my sweetest girly smile and said, "I like you too, Mr. Johnson."

I squirmed, trying hard to wriggle free, but he pressed me up against the door, kissing me, slobbering all over my face, hands feeling all over my body, pulling at my clothes.

All of a sudden, I remembered something I'd seen on TV: I hit him between his legs with my knee really hard. Mr. Sam Johnson screamed like a sissy and let go of me.

I pushed him down hard, grabbed my purse and yanked open the front door at the same time, and bolted. I pressed the elevator button three times. "Come on!" I complained loudly. Probably out of order again, so I exploded into the stairwell and stumbled down the steps.

Faster than an Olympic track star, I flew down the block and around the corner, looking back every few seconds, making sure he wasn't following me. I galloped three blocks before I pulled out my cell and called Mama. She picked up on the second ring.

I was breathing so hard I could barely talk. "Mama . . . he . . ."

"He?"

"Sam," I replied. He didn't deserve the *Mr.* anymore.

By the time the police got to our apartment, he and most of his stuff were gone. "I'd have the locks changed, if I were you," the lady police officer told Mama.

We were sitting on the couch, waiting for the locksmith, when Mama reached for my hand. I pulled it away. "Don't touch me! I hate you!"

"I'm sorry, Sunday."

"You should be." I couldn't even look at her.

"Please don't tell your daddy," she begged. "He'll have them take you away from me . . . promise?"

Unable to imagine living with that evil thing called his second wife and their two brats, I told her, "I promise," but then I let her have it. "Soon as I graduate, I'm outta this nest. I'm goin' to college as far away from you as possible, and I won't care if I ever see you again. Then your sorry ass can have any man you want!"

Mama put her hand on my shoulder. "I told you not to touch me!" I yelled. "I don't want anyone to touch me!"

I balled up my fist and was about to punch her when the doorbell rang.

Mama put her eye to the peephole. It was the locksmith.

I retreated to my room, sat down on the bed, and began to blame myself. Maybe it was those shorts I wore the other day. "It's not like they were Daisy Dukes," I whispered.

My cell rang and I jumped. It was Shante. I let it go to voice mail. I didn't want to talk to her, to anyone.

What if he comes back? What if I see him when I'm walking to school or out with my friends? What if Mama decides it's all my fault and kicks me out? Too many what ifs.

Flashing back to him slobbering on my face, I went to the bathroom and turned on the shower. I needed to wash him off. Not wanting anything he'd touched, I tore off my T-shirt and jeans and tossed them in the trash. I washed everywhere and scrubbed my face raw.

Just as I got back in my room, the doorbell rang again. Cautiously, I cracked the door and peeked. The locksmith was gone, but my granny had come over. She handed Mama something wrapped in a brown paper bag. "You need this," Granny told her.

Then Granny headed to my room and called my name softly, the way she did whenever I wasn't feeling good. "Sunday?"

Like a baby girl I replied, "Huh?"

"Can I come in?" she asked.

I opened the door, and she threw her arms around me and hugged me for a long time. "That's my smart girl," she said, and finally, I cried.

"They weren't Daisy Dukes," I whimpered.

Granny wiped at the tears on my face. "Daisy Dukes?"

"Never mind."

"It's all over, baby," she whispered, trying to comfort me.

"Yeah," I sniveled. But something told me it wasn't.

FRIDAY

DURING A FREE PERIOD, MS. HART SAT IN HER CLASSROOM grading papers. But it wasn't long before a mockingbird's song drew her to the window. The emerald fronds of a trio of palm trees were shimmering, and the sun warmed her face. Southern California was trying hard to grow on her. Tomorrow she was taking the train along the Pacific Coast to Santa Barbara, and in two weeks she was going on a wine-tasting trip to Ojai with some of her teacher friends.

She closed her eyes and basked in the silence for a moment before grabbing her coffee cup and heading to the teachers' lounge for a refill.

A few students dotted the corridors, and one of them was Sunday Waters. She'd gotten a note this morning from the office letting her know she would be out for a few days, so Ms. Hart was surprised to see her. "Hi, Sunday," Ms. Hart said. "I thought you were going to be absent."

"Oh . . . hey, Miz Hart, I only came to school to turn in my history report, and I have a pass, okay?" she replied, waving the slip of paper to defend her presence in the hall.

"No problem," Ms. Hart replied. "Everything all right?"

"Yeah. But we had to go to the police station and stuff." Sunday dropped her head, and when she looked up again, her eyes were brimming with tears.

Ms. Hart wrapped a supportive arm around Sunday's shoulder. "What happened?"

Tears trickled down her face. "I'm sorry," she said.

"For what?"

Wiping at her tears with the sleeve of her jacket, she mumbled, "For cryin'."

"Sunday, there's absolutely no need to apologize. You want to talk about it?" Ms. Hart asked.

She scanned the hall. Except for the two of them it seemed deserted. "Ain't nuthin'. . . . This man who used to live with us, who was my mama's boyfriend, tried to . . . get with me, but I fought with him so he didn't . . . you know."

"Are you okay?" Ms. Hart asked. Immediately she thought, *What a stupid question. Of course she isn't okay.*

Sunday shrugged. "My mama's waitin' outside to take me to see a psychologist. It's covered on her insurance plan."

"Oh, Sunday, you must have been terrified."

"You don't have a clue, and now I probably gotta go to court and that's what really has me messed up because I don't ever wanna see him again."

"That would be awful! Maybe they could do it by video."

She almost smiled. "They could do that?"

"I saw it on TV once."

"Thanks. I'll tell my mama." Sunday turned to walk away.

"And Sunday?" Ms. Hart added.

"Yes?"

"You're very brave."

Sunday forced a little grin. "For real, huh?"

"And don't worry about your assignments," Ms. Hart added. "You can make them up whenever you're ready."

"Thanks, Miz Hart." She started down the hall, then hesitated and added, "Don't say nuthin' to anyone, okay? Not even Shante, 'cuz I didn't tell her yet."

Ms. Hart pressed her finger to her lips.

Sunday broke into a real grin this time. "You cool, Miz Hart."

Ms. Hart was stunned. "I am?"

"Yeah. You're my favorite teacher."

"Well, thank you, Sunday," Ms. Hart said quietly. "And don't worry, everything will be okay."

The bell sounded, breaking the mood, and Sunday hurried away. Ms. Hart's eyes were watery as she ducked into the teachers' lounge.

After the encounter with Sunday, the day stretched slowly until last period arrived.

Marlon was the last to enter the classroom. He was wearing a knee brace and walking with crutches.

The room hushed. Wide eyes followed Marlon to his seat. Mary cackled to herself while Gus and Carlos gaped. Jake raised his eyebrows. Shante's hand covered her mouth.

Dorian chuckled. "Y'all can lose the worried looks. *My boy's* down but not out."

"Is it serious?" Ms. Hart asked Marlon.

"Naw, nuthin' serious." Marlon spoke with his usual confidence. "Small tear in my ACL. Having arthroscopic surgery tomorrow. Doctor said I'll be good as new, but I might miss the rest of the season."

Ms. Hart smiled. "Glad it's not too bad."

"Me too," he replied as he took his seat.

Mary hissed and others whispered.

"Quiet down, everyone," Ms. Hart said. "Let's turn to page forty-six of your literature book. It's one of my favorite short stories, 'The Winner,' by Barbara Kimenye. Who wants to read first?"

"Out loud?" Ronni asked.

"Yes, out loud. Who would like to start?"

Carlos raised his hand and had begun reading when there was a knock at the door. The principal, Mr. Garcia, cracked it open just enough to peer in. Everyone in the classroom sat up straight as he gestured for Ms. Hart to come into the hall.

"Is something wrong, Mr. Garcia?" she asked when they got outside.

"I need to see Jake Peterson. Tell him to bring his things. It's his mother. I'll wait here."

She knew Jake's mom had HIV from a journal entry he'd written once. She must be sick, Ms. Hart thought as she went back into the classroom and whispered in Jake's ear that the principal needed to talk to him.

Fear flashed in Jake's eyes. "Did I do something wrong?"

She rubbed his shoulder for reassurance. "No, nothing like that."

Hurriedly, he slung his backpack over his shoulder. But before he left, Jake turned and forced a smile at Shante. Shante smiled back, but concern was in her eyes, and Ms. Hart knew romance had bloomed.

After class Ms. Hart sat at her desk, watching the clock tick away the time. Soon she found herself thinking about Marlon—braggart or not, she hoped his leg would be okay. Her thoughts shifted to Jake's mother, and Ms. Hart tried hard to convince herself it was nothing serious. But when her mind landed on Sunday, it stayed there for a long time. Being fifteen wasn't supposed to be so hard.

COMA

(JAKE)

CUE AND MOM'S FRIEND RUBY WERE IN THE SCHOOL OFFICE when I got there. "What's going on?" I asked.

"Mom," Cue answered. "She's in the hospital. C'mon."

"But she's been fine lately—"

"It's not HIV, dude. She was in a car accident."

"A bad one," Ruby added.

As we raced to the hospital, I knew I should have been worried about Pretty Georgie. But all I could think about was our fight earlier in the week.

When Mom got home the night I asked Shante out, she must have heard me playing the keyboard. Cue's warning about how Mom might react to Shante was heavy on my mind. Determined to find out what was really going on inside Pretty Georgie's head, I'd told her that the song I was writing was for a girl I liked at school. As always,

Pretty Georgie took the bait and pressed me for more info.

"Is she nice?"

"Very," I replied.

"Is she pretty?"

"Another yes."

Pretty Georgie smiled. "What does she look like?"

"She's about your height, and she has hair to her shoulders. Her eyes are brown, and she's black."

Pretty Georgie lost the smile. "She's black?"

"Yep."

"You're joking, Jake."

I couldn't believe it. "No, Jake isn't joking. What's the next question, Mom? Can't you find a white girl?"

"Well, can't you?" she replied angrily.

"What about all that stuff you taught us growing up about how God doesn't see color and that our differences don't matter? And how having HIV taught you about prejudice because once people find out, they treat you different? What about all that?"

She tried to respond, but I didn't give her a chance.

"Why do ignorant people like you get stressed out over nonsense?" I yelled. "I hate you!" I added and stormed out of the trailer.

I hadn't spoken to her since. And now she was in the hospital.

. . .

We found Pretty Georgie in a coma in the ICU, with tubes and lines everywhere. A machine was breathing for her. Her face was so bruised and swollen that she was almost unrecognizable. Her eyes were taped shut. Pretty Georgie looked pretty bad.

I touched her small hand, which was cold as ice. "Wake up, Mom," I whimpered in her ear. Remembering this thing I'd seen on TV, I said, "Mom, if you can hear me, squeeze my hand." Nothing.

This was beyond messed up. She'd beaten HIV just to have this happen? I pictured the angel of death at her bedside determined to get her any way he could. But I wasn't about to let him win.

I bent down close. "Mom, if you can hear me, please, squeeze my hand," I begged. "I'm sorry about what I said. I don't hate you. I need you. Please."

Nothing.

Cue and Ruby stood huddled on the other side of the bed. I wanted to cry, but instead, I left the room and asked a nurse in the hallway where the chapel was. I hurried to the small candlelit room, where I dropped to my knees and prayed really hard. It had worked before when I was younger and asked for her not to die from HIV. If God had heard me once, he might hear me again.

By the time I got back to her room, visiting hours were over. "Make sure she gets her HIV medicine, okay? It's only one pill," I reminded the male nurse who was checking the respirator.

"It's taken care of," he said. "Your brother gave us her meds."

Outside, it was drizzling, and except for the sound of the windshield wipers scraping the barely wet windows, the car was silent as we drove Ruby home. Before long we pulled up to her house.

As she got out of the car, Ruby handed me an envelope. "This is for you two."

"What is it?" I asked.

"Something your mother told me to give you in case anything happened to her."

"She's gonna be fine, though," I told her and pushed it away, but Ruby dropped it in the backseat before she went inside.

"Probably insurance papers," Cue said as we rode off.

After a while I reached back for the envelope and opened it up. Like Cue said, it contained insurance papers, but there was also a picture of Pretty Georgie and our dad, Virgil, on their wedding day. Our dad had died so long ago that I hardly remembered him. They looked so happy that for a while I forgot about everything else.

Cue glanced at the photo. "Dude, don't worry—she won't die."

My eyes were dry as I imagined myself in a room full of crystal balls. Randomly, I picked one up. When I peered inside, the future looked perfect and Pretty Georgie was fine.

MJ

(Ronni)

My eyebrows need plucking, I thought as I gazed into the makeup mirror. I flipped it to the side that magnifies your image five times and started on my brows. I'm a magician with tweezers.

Suddenly there was my dad, standing in the doorway. *Didn't he have anywhere else to be?*

"Hi, Veronica—I mean Ronni," he said.

Does he always have to bother me when I'm busy?

"Can't you say hello?" he asked.

"Hell-o," I replied and continued tweezing.

He scanned my vanity and nightstands. Makeup and polish were crammed everywhere. "You have enough to start your own store, *mija*." He chuckled.

"One day I might."

He sighed. "There are more important things than beauty."

That's what you think, I wanted to say.

I checked the time on my cell and wondered where Mary was. She'd agreed to the makeover, and later, when I'd popped the question about tutoring so I could pass algebra and get the car, she'd said she'd be happy to help me.

The little genius better get here soon. My party was tomorrow, and I still had way too many things to do.

I was punching in her number on my cell when the doorbell rang. I opened the door and there she stood, as plain as a blank canvas.

"C'mon in," I told her, anxious to begin my master-piece. I grabbed her hand and led her to my room. "Sit here," I told her, motioning to the swivel chair.

"Okay," Mary said. "What's first?"

"Your before picture." I aimed my digital camera. "Hold still."

Click.

"What's next?"

I studied her eyebrows, or should I say eye-bushes. "Brows, of course." Pink tweezers in hand, I went to work.

"Ouch!" Mary flinched as I plucked.

"Don't move," I warned.

I'd perfected one brow and was admiring my work when my dad yelled from the other room, "I'm going to Target, Veronica. Anything you need?"

"No!"

"Be back soon!"

"Yeah, yeah." I started the other brow.

"Your name's Veronica?"

"Yeah."

"It's a pretty name. Why did you change it?"

"Because Ronni sounds cooler."

"And you wanted to be cool."

"I was always cool," I informed her.

"And popular?"

I smiled. "I was never unpopular."

"Maybe I should change my name," Mary said.

"To what?" I asked.

"Something with a *K* . . . like Kiley, or Kara, or—"

"You could always use your middle name."

"Jane?" she said.

"Mary Jane?" I couldn't believe it. Who does that to a kid? Then it hit me. "Your initials, MJ," I told her.

"MJ?" She grinned. "That sounds good."

Instantly, I felt proud, like I deserved a pat on the back for helping the plain Jane with the plain name. In fact, I felt so good I decided to ask her if she wanted to come to my party.

MJ looked surprised. "Me? Sure."

"Then pay real close attention to what I do because I'm going to give you some makeup so you can do it yourself at home, okay?"

"Okay," she replied and sat up straight.

"Last year, my grandmother wanted me to have a Quinceañera, but there was no way I wanted to deal with all that church stuff," I blabbed as I put on her foundation.

"What's a Quinceañera?" MJ asked.

"A big party for Latina girls when they turn fifteen. Like you're not a little girl anymore. There's a mass, and you wear a formal dress. It's kind of old school. Anyway . . . I said no way, but this year I decided to have a sixteenth birthday party."

"What should I wear?"

"Anything cute," I told her. "And wash your hair with one of those shampoos that add color. Red would be good . . . and wear your hair down. Do you have a flatiron?"

"No."

"Get one," I ordered. "Jake and Shante will be there too."

MJ shrank in the chair. "And Marlon?"

"No, he's having surgery tomorrow, remember? But maybe some other people you know, like Gus."

"Gus?"

For some reason I felt like I needed to make an excuse for inviting him. "Yeah, he lives downstairs. He's kinda sweet, plus our little-old-lady neighbor was dying and he saved her life."

"He's really shy."

"For real," I said and kept on working. Bronzer, blush, concealer, highlighter, shading, eye shadow, eyeliner, mascara, lip gloss. By the time I'd finished with Mary Jane Holly—now known as MJ—she looked amazing. I could tell she liked what she saw in the mirror.

"Thanks, Ronni," she said. "You're really good at this."

"I know," I replied. "You're still coming over Sunday night to tutor me, right? I have a test on Wednesday, and I have to pass this class. I *have* to pass."

"You will," MJ replied confidently.

"It needs tires, a brake job, and an alternator."

"The car?" she asked.

"Yeah, and a new fuel pump."

MJ looked sympathetic. "A white elephant."

"No, it's a red Honda. I've been saving the money I get from my makeovers. I almost have enough."

MJ opened her purse and pulled out some bills. "How much do I owe you?" she asked with a guilty look.

"Put your money away, *amiga*. I told you if you tutored me the makeover was free."

"So it's like bartering," MJ said.

"What's that mean?"

"To trade by exchange of commodities rather than by use of money," she rattled off like a dictionary.

I didn't understand, and it must have shown on my face.

"Like I have something you want and you have something I want, so instead of paying each other, we trade," MJ explained.

"Oh." I fluffed her hair and positioned her for the after pic. "Try to look sexy."

Click.

NO MILK, NO NUTHIN'

(DORIAN)

"NO MILK, NO NUTHIN'. NOT EVEN A SLICE OF BREAD up in here," I said and pushed the refrigerator door closed.

My three younger brothers tried to force smiles.

I picked up the phone—still disconnected. At least the lights were working.

"Where's Mama?" I asked my brothers.

"Gone to school," six-year-old Rashad answered. Our mama was studying to be a nurse.

"Someone stole the check out the mailbox, so she had to leave early to see 'bout it," nine-year-old Leon explained.

Not again, I thought. "This ain't no kinda way to live," I muttered. "Government housing, welfare, WIC."

Quinn, only four, tugged on my shirt. "I'm hungry."

"C'mon," I said, herding them toward the front door.

"Where we goin'?" Leon asked.

"To Nana's," I replied.

Once I got them outside, Leon planted himself on the porch. "You gonna get us in trouble," he said. Mama and Nana were on the outs, as usual.

"You hungry?" I asked him.

"Yeah."

"Then get your little butt up and come on."

We walked the five blocks to Nana's house quickly. By the time we got there, it was almost dark. The porch light was on at her little white house, which made me feel relieved as we walked up the path.

Rashad leaned on the doorbell, causing Nana's Chihuahua, Pepper, to bark loudly at us from behind the door.

"Hush up, dog," our grandmother called as she pulled back the curtains and peeked out. "Who's there?"

"Us, Nana . . . and we're hungry," Leon shouted.

We heard Nana unlocking the door. "You the loudest mouthed, just like that no 'count calls hisself your daddy. Get your narrow butts in here b'fore you have the whole block in my bizness."

"Sorry," I explained, "but they're hungry and Mama wasn't home and the check didn't come or got stolen and we're all out of food stamps."

"She at school?" Nana asked.

We nodded. "She can't miss no more classes," Leon explained.

Nana took Quinn up in her arms. "College at her age.

Oughtta go on back to the Wal-Mart. Coulda made manager by now. Y'all want catfish or chicken?"

"Don't matter," I replied.

"I want French fries!" Leon shouted from the front room, where he was already plopped in front of the TV.

"Me too," Rashad echoed.

"College at her age," Nana repeated.

I wanted to tell Nana that Mama wasn't that old. She was only thirty-seven. Plus she had only one more semester until she'd be a real registered nurse. Then we'd move up out the Section Eight building, on to something better, maybe into our own house. But I held my tongue.

I butted through the screen door into the backyard, sat down on the steps, and stared up as the first few stars began to dot the sky. They made me think about my class assignment. I laughed: "A Star on the Hollywood Walk of Fame"? All I wanted right now was dinner.

Through the open door, I could hear Nana talking to Quinn, who was sitting on a stool beside her at the sink. "No 'count, shiftless, triflin'. Warned her not to marry that'n. All the nice young fellas who came callin' after Shonda. Coulda had any one of 'em, but she settles on a criminal. I knew he'd wind up behind bars. Had that no-class street look. And always clownin' . . . makin' fun of folks, everything a joke."

Always the same old story. I wished she would shut up. But her words made me wonder: "Always clownin' . . .

makin' fun of folks, everything a joke." No, I'm nothing like him, I told myself.

There was about a minute of quiet before Nana started up again, "Now she all high-minded . . . college."

This kind of bad talk was why my mama and Nana weren't speaking. I didn't mind the talk about my daddy—there wasn't too much good that anyone could say about him. But when Nana started in on my mama, I got mad.

I threw open the screen door and strode inside. "Why you gotta always be like that? Talkin' her down?"

Nana was peeling potatoes with a knife. She looked up and pointed the knife at me. "Respect me, boy."

I wasn't about to back down. "I ain't no boy, and I ain't scared a you, old lady. You ain't got no sense noway."

"I'm hungry," Quinn whined from his stool.

Nana waved the knife in the air like a crazy person. "I ain't gotta feed none a y'all. Cain't respect me, get the hell out my house!"

I grabbed Quinn and sprang into the next room. Nana flew after me, waving the knife. Rashad saw the knife and dashed out the front door faster than a bullet. The rest of us were on his heels.

"No 'counts just like your daddy!" was the last thing Nana shouted before she slammed the door.

"Are not," Leon whispered as we stood on the sidewalk.

Rashad looked at me. "I'm still hungry," he said.

Now what? We made our way toward home through the dark streets. A mean old man who was watering his lawn threatened to wet us if we stepped on his grass, and a few cars rolled by with the music bumpin' loudly, but mostly everything was quiet.

We were passing in front of a 7-Eleven when a bad thought entered my mind. We could easily steal something to eat—bread, chips, anything. I tried to push the thought out, but it wouldn't go away. I glanced back toward where Nana lived, her words repeating over and over like a broken record. "No 'counts just like your daddy . . . triflin' . . . always clownin', makin' fun of folks," and shook my head.

But the "always clownin', makin' fun of folks" bothered me. Clowning and dissing are the two things I'm really good at. People pay attention to me when I clown and diss. I held Quinn tight as we trudged through the neighborhood. For the first time in a long time, I was nothing but serious.

Leon picked up an empty beer can. "Hey, Dorian, we could collect bottles and cans like them homeless people. Or we could beg for money by the freeway or outside McDonald's or Burger King."

"Okay, but only this one time," I told them. "I'm gonna get a job to help Mama. But tonight we gotta eat." We changed direction and headed to McDonald's.

We stood near the drive-thru, Quinn holding a discarded plastic soda cup that had a picture of Ronald Mc-Donald on it.

"We didn't have no dinner," Rashad told the first person who went through the line. The guy dropped a quarter in the cup and drove ahead to pick up his food.

One quarter, I thought. This is going to take all night.

The next customer was more generous. A handful of spare change.

"You all are hungry, aren't you?" the third asked. She was a little old lady who looked like she was on her way home from church. I eyed the Bible on the dashboard of her car.

"I am," Rashad answered. "And my stomach's makin' noises too."

"Wait here. I'll be right back," she said.

It seemed like a very long time, and I wondered if she was really coming back. But once she parked her car, she came back to the drive-thru window on foot and led us inside McDonald's.

"Order whatever you want," she told us.

"Even fries?" Leon asked.

"Even fries," she replied.

"Say thank you," I reminded my brothers.

Rashad, Leon, and Quinn all chorused "Thank you!" together at the top of their lungs.

She sat with us while we ate and drank, watching over us like she was some kind of angel. "Where's your mother?" she asked.

"At school," I said proudly between bites of my Big Mac. "She's studying to be a nurse. And she's 'bouta graduate."

Leon fed her the rest of the story. "And we ain't never begged for food before, but Dorian said we had to because we ran out of stamps and someone stole our check."

"Welfare?" the woman asked.

Suddenly, I felt ashamed. I wanted to spit out the food in my mouth. Instead I swallowed and to keep some dignity replied, "Only since she's been in school. Before that, she had a regular job at Wal-Mart. She could have been a manager by now if she'd stayed."

The old church lady smiled at me. "You live near here?"

"Not far, three blocks," Leon answered.

"I'll drive you home," she said. "Nice boys like you shouldn't be out walking at this time."

Nice boys, I thought as I watched my brothers dipping fries into ketchup and then chewing with their mouths closed like Mama taught us. We are nice boys. Not no 'counts. Not criminals. Not triflin'.

We all thanked her again as we climbed out of her car. "You all tell your mother to come to church, she ever needs help. The big one on the corner of Eighteenth Street."

"I will," I replied. "And thank you."

"My name's Mrs. Hobson," she said, then added, "and tell your mother she has four fine sons."

"I will and thank you again, Miz Hobson."

I saw her watching us from the curb until we got inside before driving away.

As I closed the door, I thought about my daddy again. I wasn't trying to have a jacked-up life like him, so I decided then and there to stop playing the fool. It wasn't going to be easy to stop clowning and dissing folks because I'm so good at it. But begging had made me feel like a piece of nothing.

I dug around in my backpack and pulled out the book we were supposed to be reading in Ms. Hart's class, *The Old Man and the Sea*. A report was due next week, and I hadn't even opened the book. I turned to page one and started to read.

I was a few pages in when Mama opened the door, holding a bucket of KFC and all of the fixings.

"We ain't hungry," Rashad said, yawning.

Mama's face became a question mark.

"It's a long story," I replied and flipped to the next page.

ONE BULLET

(SUNDAY)

THE CREAKING SOUND OF SOMEONE OPENING THE DOOR TO MY room woke me, and I leaped up out of bed.

"Sorry, Sunday," Mama apologized. "I didn't mean to scare you. I have to go out for a few minutes, but I'll be right back."

I ignored her, crawled back into bed, and pulled the covers over my head.

It had been a few days and Mama kept trying to be all nice, but I still couldn't look her in the eyes. When I heard her leave the apartment, I grabbed the butcher knife I'd hidden under my bed and went to the front door to check the locks. For the first time since it'd happened, I was alone.

From the living room window, I watched the streets, wondering where Mama had gone. My mind flipped to Shante, who had left me a gazillion messages, wondering if something was wrong. I was about to call her when I noticed the crumpled brown paper wrapping on the table. It was from the package Granny had given Mama that night. I forgot about calling Shante and went searching for what had been inside.

I looked under Mama's bed. It wasn't there. One by one, I searched her drawers and finally, the closet. When I saw the shoe box on the top shelf, I knew that was where she'd put it. She never kept her shoes up there.

Standing on a chair, I swiped at it, missed, and almost lost my balance. I tried again. Got it!

Like I'd figured, it was a gun.

At first I felt afraid to touch it, so I just stared. Though it was shiny and silver like one of those toy cowboy guns, I knew it was real. I picked it up and thought, Wow, it's heavy. I turned the wheel thing around the way I'd seen them do on TV and looked for the bullets. There was only one. "One bullet," I said out loud.

Suddenly, I heard noises. Someone was at the front door, trying to unlock it. Still holding the gun, I crept to the door and put my eye to the peephole. It was Mr. Johnson.

"Oh, shit," I whispered. He must have thought we weren't home.

He jiggled the key again. Quietly, I backed away and tiptoed toward the phone to call the cops. But the sound of Mama's voice in the hallway brought me to a halt.

"You molested my child!" she screamed.

"This is all a misunderstandin'. . . . All I want is my things, woman!" Mr. Johnson yelled back.

"Get the hell away from here!" Mama shrieked.

The sound of scuffling led me back to the door. When I peeped again, Mama and Mr. Johnson were hitting each other. I cracked open the door to help, but Mama commanded, "Lock the door, Sunday, and call 911!"

As I made the call, I heard Mama gasp, "Jesus, help me!" I dropped the phone and peeped again. This time Mr. Johnson had Mama on the ground, and he was choking her!

I threw open the door and pointed the gun at him. "Get off her!" Out of the corner of my eye, I saw one of our old-lady neighbors peeking through her door.

Mr. Johnson let go of Mama's neck and lunged at me. That was when the gun went off. The next thing I knew, he was on the ground, holding his stomach where the bullet had hit him, the blood quickly turning his white shirt red. I heard sirens. Someone else must have called the cops.

"You shot me," he moaned.

Mama grabbed her purse and a small box that must have fallen out of it, then led me back inside the apartment. We were both shaking. There were red marks around her neck from where he'd choked her, and her nose was bleeding. My hand felt frozen to the gun. "Let me have it, Sunday," she said.

"One bullet," I said.

"I know," she replied as she placed the box on the table. The writing on the box said AMMUNITION. "I know, Sunday," she repeated and we both started crying.

When the cops showed up a few minutes later with the paramedics, I asked two questions:

Is Mr. Johnson gonna die?

Am I going to juvie?

MARLY

(MARLON)

WHEN I WOKE UP AFTER SURGERY, MOMS AND POPS were standing beside the bed. I was still hooked up to the IV, which this nurse was adjusting. I tried to talk, but my voice felt scratchy. Moms took my hand and gave me a weak smile.

"Are you having any pain?" the nurse asked.

I shook my head no.

Pops had a strange look on his face.

I reached down and touched my knee, which was heavily bandaged. I coughed a few times and cleared my throat enough to ask, "What's wrong?"

"It's worse than they thought," Pops replied. "One of the menisci was damaged. They did the best they could but—"

The best they could? "Am I gonna be able to play ball?"

Moms squeezed my hand. "Definitely not this season," Pops replied.

Okay, that much I'd figured, but something I saw in his eyes told me there was more to the story. "And?" I asked.

Moms squeezed my hand tighter and whispered, "They found something . . . a growth on your bone."

I listened in shock as Pops explained. "It was small, but after the doctor took the biopsy, he decided to remove it anyway. Even if it's not something serious, he said he didn't want to give it a chance to grow because the bone can get weak and you run the risk of a pathological fracture."

"But the MRI only showed an ACL tear," I said weakly.

Pops rested his hand on my shoulder. "It also showed a growth, but we didn't want to upset you in case it turned out to be nothing."

"Cancer?" I asked.

Moms started crying.

My pops' voice got quivery. "The doctor won't know until he gets the pathology result."

This had to be a dream. I shut my eyes tight, but when I opened them, my moms and pops were still standing there with these pitiful looks on their faces. My stomach started to cramp, but there was nothing inside it to puke.

Oh, hell no, I thought. I pushed away my moms' hand. "Do I have to stay here?"

"No, sweetheart. The doctor said you can leave as soon as you feel okay."

After we got home, I tried to fall asleep to forget all about it. The phone rang, and Moms knocked on the door. "It's your brother. He wants to talk to you."

Angry thoughts collided inside my head. I grabbed the phone from her hand. "Kiss my ass, asshole!" I yelled into the phone, then hurled it to the floor. I glared at my mother. "And you can get out of my face!"

But she wouldn't leave. "Are you having pain, Marlon?" she asked, approaching the bed. "It's been several hours since you had a pain pill."

Maybe it was the way she didn't get mad at me for yelling, but I couldn't hold back my tears any longer.

She sat on the edge of the bed. My head found her lap, and I cried like a baby boy. "Why me?" I asked.

"You're going to be fine, Marly," she said.

She hadn't called me Marly since I was eight or nine. It made me feel a little better. Like her love for me could make it right. That's what love does, doesn't it? Makes everything right?

PARTY TIME

(GUS)

THE PAST SEVENTY-TWO HOURS OF MY LIFE HAD been a countdown to the day of Ronni's party, and now that it was finally here, I felt petrified. It seemed like things had changed between us, because now she smiled at me in the halls at school and said hi, and one time when I ran into her at our apartment building, she asked how Miz Rosenthal was doing. But she always had at least two or three big jocks around her at school, so who was I kidding to think she would ever feel about me the way I felt about her? So much for my stupid Cupid fantasy.

"Is it okay if I come in with you?" my mom asked as we pulled up to the Elks Lodge where Ronni was having her party. "Just to say hello?"

I gave her a look as if to say, You have to be joking. Before she came to a complete stop, I opened the door.

"I'll pick you up at midnight," she called after me as I rushed to the entrance.

"Who do I look like, Cinderella?" I shouted back at her.

"Twelve thirty, then. . . . I have to work tomorrow, remember?"

"Okay, twelve thirty, but don't come inside. I'll meet you out here, all right?" Mercifully, she started the car and drove away.

A tall, muscular guy was blocking the door. I could hear Latin music blasting from inside. "What's your name?" he demanded.

"Gus Little," I replied and handed him the invitation.

He snatched it from my hand and smirked as he searched the list. Why did my last name have to be Little? Lots of people had promised me a growth spurt. Was I going to be five-two forever? Maybe I should eat more.

A huge knot of people was hovering near the door. I weaved my way through and finally got inside. My first scan of the room came up empty—no Ronni. I tried standing on tiptoes to see, but it was useless, so I went over to the food table.

As I loaded my plate with hors d'oeuvres and other stuff, trying to jump-start the long-predicted growth spurt, I heard someone behind me say, "Hey, Gus."

I turned around. It was Mary from class. She was wearing makeup, and she had her hair down. I almost didn't recognize her.

"You can close your mouth now," she said.

"You look different," I told her between bites of shrimp.

Mary smiled. "I know. Ronni made me over."

She eyed the pile of food on my plate.

"Everyone keeps telling me to eat more so I'll grow," I said.

She laughed. "Everyone keeps telling me the exact opposite."

"But you're losing weight."

"You can tell?"

My mouth was full, so I nodded. That seemed to make Mary happy—I don't think I'd ever seen her look happy before.

"I didn't know you and Ronni were friends," I said. For some reason I didn't feel shy around Mary.

"Only sort of friends. It's a symbiotic relationship. She'd been harassing me about doing a makeover on me, and I finally said okay. She did a really good job, huh?"

After swallowing the bite in my mouth, I replied, "Yeah, she really did."

The music had changed to hip-hop, and lots of people were on the dance floor. Mary started moving to the music, and I could tell she wanted to dance. I decided why not? I put down my plate. "You wanna dance?" I asked her.

She stared at me in surprise. "You're messing with me, right?"

"No, it's one of my favorite songs. C'mon."

Mary may have been plump, but she could move. She did these Egyptian-like moves with her arms, and I mimicked her. We were having so much fun that I almost forgot about Ronni until I saw her across the room.

She was in the middle of the floor, wearing a gold miniskirt and a matching strapless top. She was dancing with this All-League senior football player.

I stared at Ronni until I caught her eye. She smiled and gave me her standard finger wave. The football player pulled her close like she belonged to him, and she kissed his ear.

Right then, I accepted the truth—a finger wave and a smile was the best I could ever expect from her. My gut ached, like someone had socked me. Hard.

"You okay, Gus?" Mary seemed concerned.

"Uh, I ate too much," I said.

The song had ended, so I led her from the dance floor.

"Did you know Ronni's real name is Veronica?" she asked.

"Yeah, her father still calls her that." I paused before divulging, "My real name is Augustus."

"Augustus Caesar, 63 B.C. to A.D. 14. Did you know that when he died, the Roman Senate declared him a god?" Mary spouted.

I knew some stuff about him, but not that. "No," I replied.

"And his real name was Gaius Octavius."

She must have an encyclopedia inside her head, I thought. *And she's easy to talk to.*

Mary kept going. "You know, Ronni thought up a new name for me."

"A new name?"

"Yeah, it's MJ."

"Why MJ?" I asked.

"For Mary Jane."

"Hey, you must be Roman, too!" I told her. We both laughed.

When the music started up again, we headed back to the floor. And as MJ and I danced to song after song, my Ronni fantasies began to fizzle.

BEST FRIENDS

(SUNDAY)

THE MORNING AFTER I SHOT MR. JOHNSON, I FELT WORSE THAN terrible, but I decided I absolutely had to call Shante. In five years we'd never gone longer than twenty-four hours without talking. Now it'd been almost three whole days since my best friend and I had spoken.

"Finally," she said when she answered the phone.

"Hey," I replied.

"What's wrong?" Shante asked. "Where've you been? Are you sick or something?"

I felt like blurting out the whole story, but instead I lied. "Yeah, I'm sick."

"Oh, I thought something real bad musta happened because you didn't call me back or text me or anything, and the phone at your house said the number was no longer in service. And if you hadn't called me tonight, I planned to ask my daddy to check with the police." There was a pause. "You still mad?" she asked softly.

Mad? About what? So much had happened over the past few days. Then I remembered. "Oh, about white boy?"

"His name is Jake, not white boy."

Here we go again, with Shante's love life, like it's the only important thing in the world. We'd been on the phone only a few minutes, but I really didn't feel like talking about Shante's latest romantic drama. So I was glad when Mama knocked on my door. "Sunday?"

"Hold on a minute," I said to Shante.

"I cooked breakfast," Mama said.

"Not hungry," I said, even though I really was.

"Strawberry waffles . . . your favorite."

I smelled the food through the open door and my mouth started to water. "Bacon?"

"Yes."

"Okay, I'm comin'. Shante, I gotta go. Breakfast."

"I'll call you back in one hour. I have a lot to tell you."

Mama and I didn't have much to say, and as we ate, the apartment was quiet. The picture of Mr. Johnson's blood-stained shirt kept flashing through my mind. I couldn't stop remembering the way the gun had felt when it fired, the look in his eyes that said, *I can't believe this.*

I really couldn't believe it either, and so I broke the silence and asked Mama, "Did I shoot Mr. Johnson?"

"Yes, Sunday."

"Oh . . . I hoped maybe I dreamed it."

"It's not a dream."

"But it should be," I said, giving her big-time attitude as I grabbed my plate and headed to my room to finish eating.

"I'm sorry, Sunday," Mama said for what seemed like the millionth time as she followed me to my room. But this time she added something that she hadn't before. "It'll never happen again, I promise. I made a mistake. I love you."

Something about the way she said it made it sound like she meant it. I stopped in my tracks and glanced back at her. She was sobbing.

I went to her. "It's okay, Mama." We hugged tightly. "Don't cry. I love you too."

When Shante called back, I let her fill me up with gossip about Marlon having to have surgery, Jake's mom being in a car accident and that being the reason she didn't go to Ronni's party, how she was thinking about trying out for a summer dance program in New York. Questions followed: How long was I going to trip about the white boy? Should she invite the white boy to her house or did I think her daddy would have a fit? Did I think the white boy's mother would like her?

I answered every question with an "I don't know."

"You're not in a very good mood, are you?" she said.

"You noticed," I replied sarcastically.

"Do you have the flu or something?"

I had to tell her. "No . . . I shot someone."

Shante laughed. "You so crazy."

"No, I'm not. I shot my mama's boyfriend."

There was silence until she asked, "Mr. Johnson?"

"Yeah."

"Did he die?"

"No, and according to the police, he's not going to," I replied. "He's in the hospital jail ward."

Quickly, I spilled my guts. When I finished, Shante said, "I cannot believe this."

"Me neither. At first I thought I'd wind up in juvie because the police were actin' like they didn't believe me and Mama, but our old-lady neighbor saw the whole thing. She's white, so you know they took her word."

Shante sighed loudly. "You wanna come to my house for dinner tonight?" she asked sympathetically. Sunday dinner at Shante's house was a soul food party. Plus, except for Hayley, the Queen Bee, I liked being around her family, so I said okay. But I didn't want to leave Mama all alone and I asked if she could come too. Shante asked her daddy and he said yes.

Later that day, before we left for Shante's house, I stared at the ceiling, thinking about how my universe would be if I, Sunday Waters, were in charge. First, my mama and daddy would never have split up and they would be really nice like Shante's parents. Second, I would have a big brother like Shante's brother Kyle to watch out for me and we would get along real good. Third, Shante would be my sister instead of my best friend. Fourth, my granny would win the lottery and move us all to Beverly Hills or Newport Beach. Fifth, for my sixteenth birthday next year I would get a brand-new white Lexus coupe with a tan leather interior. Sixth, I would get all A's without even having to study. And last, I would have a fine boyfriend who treated me with respect and stuff.

How come we can't do that, make our lives all perfect? Why can't everything and everyone be nice? How come bad things have to happen? How come?

Washing Dishes

(Carlos)

My break had just started, and I was lounging in back of the restaurant. "Is this what you call a *J-O-B*?" someone asked loudly. There stood Dorian, dressed nice in a button-down white shirt and brown pants.

"Wha's up?"

"Nothin', my man. I need a job, thought maybe you could hook me up washin' dishes or whatever. Dropped by to check it out."

"You must be psychic or something because the other dishwasher quit a half hour ago. The lady who hires is here. I could ask her. C'mon."

Dorian trailed me inside, through the kitchen to the restaurant manager's tiny office. I knocked on the half-open door.

"Miss Dobbs?"

"Yes, Carlos?" she replied.

"I have a friend who wants the dishwashing job."

She was busy on the computer and didn't look up. "Can he come by tomorrow?"

"He's here right now," I said, pushing the door open so she could see Dorian.

He introduced himself. "Dorian Green, ma'am."

Miss Dobbs put her hand out for him to shake it, and he did. "Nice to meet you," she said.

Dorian spoke properly. "Nice to meet you too, Miss Dobbs."

"Ever worked in a restaurant before?" she asked.

"No, ma'am, but I have three little brothers, so I'm good at washing dishes."

Miss Dobbs smiled and handed Dorian an application. "Fill this out. Can you work weekends?"

"Yes, ma'am," Dorian answered.

She went back to typing on her computer but kept talking. "It's minimum wage. That okay?"

"Yes, ma'am."

Miss Dobbs stared up at Dorian's face. "Ever been in trouble?"

"No, ma'am."

"Good. After you fill out the application, I'll look it over and call you. But plan on starting next weekend. Be here Saturday, eleven A.M. Carlos can train you. Wear a white shirt and black slacks. We'll give you an apron."

"Thank you, Miss Dobbs."

"Thank *you*, Dorian."

"Dawg, that was too easy," Dorian said as I led him through the kitchen to find a counter where he could fill out the application. "Thanks, Carlos."

"I didn't know you could talk like that," I told him.

Dorian laughed. "You mean proper? I got all kinda skills."

As usual at dinnertime, the restaurant was getting really busy. The chef, his cooks, the servers were darting around everywhere.

"This place be hectic," Dorian commented after he finished the application and took it back to Miss Dobbs. "Any black folks work up in here?"

"No."

"I didn't think so, 'cuz the cooks are all Latino and the bus boys too. Only that head chef guy is white," Dorian observed. "Don't get mad or nuthin', but some of my peeps won't shut up 'bout y'all takin' all the jobs, even though some of y'all ain't even got papers."

"We didn't take all the jobs," I huffed. "If they really wanted to close the borders, they would have a long time ago. It's all about money, dude. A lot of them pay undocumented workers less. Plus no health insurance, and all that equals more money in Mr. Businessman's pocket."

"You through?" Dorian asked.

I sighed, "Yeah."

"Good, 'cuz me and you, we cool. And I see your point. Thanks again for hookin' me up. Time for me to help my moms with finances. See ya tomorrow."

We butted knuckles and he was gone.

After Dorian left, I scrubbed the rest of the dishes and thought about what he had said about having jobs and not being U.S. citizens. I knew there were a lot of people who felt that way, but most of them wouldn't say it to our faces.

That night I'd just laid down on the sofa bed in the living room and shut my eyes when my father got home. He flipped on the light and started rattling around in the kitchen for food like he usually does. I rolled over and pulled the blanket over my head. I couldn't wait until I finally had my own room.

"Carlos?" he said.

"*Qué?*" I groaned.

"*Cómo estás, mijo?*"

"I'm good."

"I've been thinking about going back to Guatemala."

"For a vacation?" I asked.

"No, to live."

My eyes flew open wide. "*Qué?*" I asked again, wondering if I was hearing things.

He took a long time to answer. "I said we might have to go back to live in Guatemala."

I sat up on the couch. "We? *Por qué?*"

"Tonight my boss said the government's going to crack down harder on undocumented immigrants. There've been more and more raids. Someone said he might have to fire us all."

"But that's not fair. . . . You've been working in that body shop for ten years!"

"I know. But I keep hearing things about deportation. I'm getting worried."

He's getting worried? I don't believe this. "So why don't you try to get your green card? Then you'd be legal. Your boss can do something called a labor certification request. All the information is on the Internet. I've been telling you for two years, but you haven't listened. And what about the house in Lancaster?"

"I can still get most of the deposit back." He sounded like he'd already made up his mind. "That much money will buy a lot of land in our country."

"*Our country?* I haven't been back to Guatemala even once, and Julian's never been there." I folded my arms. "*This* is my country. You can go if you want to, but I'm not leaving LA."

"It's only an idea, *mijo.*"

No quiero escucharlo, I thought. I don't want to listen to him.

He put his plate into the sink, then turned off the light and headed to his room. "Go back to sleep, *mijo.*"

I tossed and turned, trying to get comfortable, but I couldn't. Visions of the house and dreams of having my own room vanished.

It's not fair, I thought. I'm not going anywhere. I'm staying right here.

THINGS CHANGE

THAT MONDAY, MARY WAS THE FIRST TO ENTER CLASS.
She had her long hair down and was wearing makeup. "You look pretty, Mary," Ms. Hart told her. And for the first time all year, Mary smiled.

Jake and Marlon were both absent. Ms. Hart promised herself she'd call them at home after school.

"So how are your journals coming?" she asked the class once everyone was seated.

"Fine," several of them moaned.

"I'm already finished," Shante said proudly.

Once Ms. Hart began teaching, she realized that Dorian was keeping quiet. He was never quiet. Dorian and snide remarks were like fire and heat—one always came with the other. Throughout the class, she found herself anticipating a joke or rude comment, but he sat at his desk, paying close attention, totally serious, maybe a little sad. And when the time came to read some poetry, Dorian's hand popped up.

"What's wrong, Dorian?" Ms. Hart asked.

"Nuthin'. . . . I wanna read."

Mary asked out loud what Ms. Hart was thinking. "Will the real Dorian please stand up?"

Dorian ignored her, not even glancing her way, and started to read aloud.

Something was wrong. Ms. Hart decided that she and Dorian needed to talk.

By the time everyone took a turn reading, the end-of-class bell had sounded. Dorian was heading quickly to the door when Ms. Hart called to him.

"Dorian, you have a minute?" she asked.

"Yeah, I got a few." He hovered near her desk as the rest of the class emptied out into the hallway.

"You forgot to give us homework," Carlos informed her on his way out.

"I didn't forget," she told him. "You guys deserve a break."

"For real!" Ronni said.

Carlos grinned at Dorian and told him, "Later."

Sunday was the last out, but before leaving, she turned and gave Ms. Hart a big smile.

"You want to sit down, Dorian?" she asked.

"Naw. . . . Sumthin' wrong?" he asked.

"That's what I wanted to ask you. I mean, today you seem different—quiet."

Dorian went over to the window and stared outside. "Oh . . . you mean 'cuz I'm not clownin' and all that?"

"Partly. But you seem a little sad too," she replied, joining him across the room.

"I ain't sad or nuthin'. Just decided to stop actin' a fool all the time."

Ms. Hart knew there had to be a story. "Did something happen?" she asked.

"I don't know if I should tell you this, 'cuz it's kinda embarrassin'." Dorian hesitated. "My pops is incarcerated. Did I ever tell you that?"

She shook her head no.

"And I have three little brothers."

Ms. Hart listened intently.

"Anyway, one day last week my mama had to go to school and we didn't have no food . . ."

A half hour passed while Dorian told her the whole story.

"Is this the first time that's happened?" Ms. Hart asked.

"Naw, it's happened before but not a lot. Usually my nana woulda fed us, but like I told you, she was in one of her moods."

Ms. Hart sighed. "You know we have school social workers who can help."

"I know, but I don't need folks at school all up in my life. B'sides, we got a government social worker."

"I could buy you some groceries, then."

"Naw . . . Miz Hart. You ain't gotta worry. My mama got her WIC and all that, plus Carlos hooked me up and I got a job so now I'll be able to help her out some."

Ms. Hart patted his shoulder. "Well, good luck, Dorian," she said. "And let me know if you guys are ever out of food again."

"It ain't gonna happen again, now that I got that job. But thanks anyway." Dorian was walking out the door when he halted and added, "You cool, Miz Hart."

Ms. Hart beamed.

"Oh . . . and I talked to the counselor today, and she told me I should take your composition class next year."

"I'm not sure I'll be here next year, Dorian."

"Why?" he asked.

"I might go back to New York City."

"NYC? And miss all this sunshine? You better not," he told her as he headed down the hall. "A'ight?"

"Bye, Dorian," she replied as the door closed behind him.

Immediately, she regretted telling him about her plans.

Thinking she might not be here next year could give the students license to stop taking her seriously, and her classes might become a free-for-all. Ms. Hart hurried down the hall to ask him not to say anything to anyone. But Dorian was gone, and there was no taking it back now.

ALL HIS FAULT

(MARLON)

ON THE WAY TO THE HOSPITAL FOR MORE TESTS, Moms patted my shoulder from the backseat. I felt pity in her touch and pulled away. I didn't want anyone's pity. What I wanted was for this to be a nightmare and for me to wake up soon.

Life is really trying to jack me up, I thought as they slid me into the MRI tube. This time it was for a total body scan.

"Stay perfectly still or we'll have to repeat it," the lady technician warned me.

It felt like I was in a tomb. I pictured myself as one of those Egyptian pharaohs buried in my own little pyramid. A tear trickled down the side of my face. I reached up to wipe it away, but the lady repeated, "Stay perfectly still."

The first tests had shown something abnormal, and the doctors said it was either a fibrous cortical defect or osteosarcoma. If it turned out to be the first one, everything was going to be cool. But osteosarcoma is bone cancer, and depending on how advanced it is, sometimes the only option is amputation.

After the scan they were going to do another biopsy.

"Stay perfectly still," the technician repeated again.

"Go to hell," I whispered.

A few of my teachers, including Ms. Hart, had called, and my coaches and all of my teammates had come by. And some of my lovelies had sent me red roses, little stuffed animals, like teddy bears and a penguin, and get-well cards they'd kissed, leaving lipstick imprints. They all said they were praying. My grandfather, a Methodist minister in Baltimore, said he had his entire congregation on their knees.

As for me, lately I'd begun to wonder if God was even for real. And if He was, the only thing I had to say to Him was, "I hate You."

"If this turns out to be cancer, no way are they cutting off my leg," I told my pops after we left the hospital. "Just put me in the ground."

Pops replied, "Okay, Marlon," like he was giving me lip service.

We'd been home only a few minutes when Chris got in from the airport. According to Moms, he was so worried about me he flew home from Yale. He was the last person I wanted to see. So when he came over to the sofa where I was resting and tried to talk to me, I grabbed my crutches and limped to my room. He followed me in, and I glared at him. "I'd like to be alone, if you don't mind."

"I want to talk," he said.

I sat on my bed. "So, talk."

"How's it going?" he asked.

"That the best you can do, big brother?"

"I want us to be friends, Marlon."

"Ain't gonna happen."

"I want to—"

I butted in. "Nuthin' but bullshit from you for the last five years, and now you wanna be friends? Why'd you really come here?"

"I'm worried about you."

"You're worried 'bout me? Don't you have to get good grades so you can be a Rhodes Scholar? Why don't you get on a red-eye back to Yale and worry 'bout that?"

Chris raised his voice. "Please hear me out."

"Speak!"

"I don't blame you for being pissed at me. I haven't been the best brother—"

"Guilty as charged," I interrupted.

"I was immature."

"Double guilty."

"And insecure," he added.

"Three strikes."

Chris stood up. "Can I finish?"

I nodded.

"I know you're going to think I'm lying, but I'm proud of you. I tell most people I meet about my brother the basketball star . . . how you're going to be famous. But maybe this thing with your leg happened for a reason. You're smart, Marlon. Basketball's good, but you can be anything. It's not the end of the world if you can't play pro ball. Don't forget that. For the record, I love you and I hope it's not cancer. That's all I have to say."

"Good. Now, get the hell out my room! Soundin' soft like some sissy! I hate your ass!"

Chris got up to leave as Moms cracked the door open. "Don't upset him, Chris."

"Yeah, don't upset me!" I blasted.

Chris left and Moms came over to my bed and caressed my head. "It's not his fault, Marlon. Get some rest."

That night I couldn't fall asleep. I stared at the slivers of light coming through the blinds from the streetlamp outside and thought, This is his fault. He's totally to blame. If I'd never played ball, this thing with my leg would be bad, like a major accident, but not a fatal collision.

I started remembering all the great stuff I'd done with basketball: stands packed with crowds yelling my name, teammates patting my back then lifting me high in the air, award ceremonies, gorgeous honeys everywhere, the places I'd been, newspaper stories, all the fun I'd had.

It was all his fault.

ON THE BUS

(SUNDAY)

WEDNESDAY AFTER SCHOOL, I CLIMBED ONTO THE BUS BEHIND Shante. We were going to meet Jake at the hospital where his mom was in the ICU. "Thanks for comin' with me," she said as we scooted into seats.

"Ain't nuthin'. You really like him, huh?" I asked.

"He's kinda cool," Shante replied.

"For a white boy," I reminded her.

"Why are you still trippin'? Race doesn't matter. Besides, there's only one race, the human race. Plus the world is changin'. Case in point, President Obama."

I stared out the window. "You keep dreamin'. President Obama or not . . . white folks ain't changed that much. Some of 'em still don't even want black neighbors. You need to get real."

"Well, I'm not gonna stop likin' him, so you need to get over it, okay?"

"Whatever."

The bus was moving fast, and Shante was watching the street signs out the window. "We're movin' in with my granny," I told her.

"Do you want to?" Shante asked.

"I s'poze so. She has bars on her windows and this alarm system, and Mama can't bring any men there 'cuz my granny's not havin' it."

Suddenly there was a loud noise, a car backfiring. I jumped, remembering the sound of the gun going off. Shante put her head on my shoulder. "You're still scared, huh? I know I would be."

"Yeah. I keep thinking he's gonna show up at our door again. I wish we had the gun, but the police took it."

"Ask your granny to buy another one," she said.

"I did, but she and my mama both said no 'cuz I coulda got shot instead of him. And the police officers kept repeatin' over and over, 'This coulda turned out very different.'"

I knew they were right. I pictured myself in Mr. Johnson's place on the ground, bleeding from a gunshot wound. "Plus the psychologist made Mama promise. No more guns."

"Maybe they'll keep him in jail for a long time, then you won't have to be afraid anymore."

"Yeah, maybe," I said, but inside it seemed like I'd be scared forever.

We pulled up to Eighteenth Street. Shante grabbed my hand. "C'mon, this is our stop."

We took the hospital's elevator to the seventh floor and followed the arrows to the ICU. There was a sign at the entrance that said to ring the bell for assistance. A woman answered. "Can I help you?"

"We're looking for Mrs. Peterson," Shante replied.

"She's not here."

Shante and I locked eyes, and I knew she was wondering if Jake's mom had died. But the woman added, "She's on the second floor."

We headed back to the elevator. When the elevator doors opened on the second floor, there was Jake. And before we were out of the elevator, he blurted out, "She woke up this morning. She's gonna be okay."

Shante hugged him. "I am so happy."

Jake held her close like she really mattered to him. Then he noticed me and said, "Hey, Sunday."

"Hey," I replied, but I began to feel strange—like I didn't belong. So when we got to the door of his mom's room, I told them, "I'm 'bouta head home, y'all."

"You don't have to leave," Shante told me as she reached to hold Jake's hand.

Jake agreed, "Yeah, we could go to the cafeteria. The food's really not that bad."

"Naw. That's okay," I replied, glancing outside. It

looked like any minute the dark gray clouds were going to let loose. "I should go before it starts rainin'."

"My brother could drive you," Jake offered.

Right then, a tall white guy with a shaved head came out of the room and spoke to Jake. "Hey, dude, Mom's asleep." His eyes quickly landed on Jake and Shante's clasped hands. I wanted to say I told you so to Shante right then and there but decided I'd wait until later.

Jake opened his mouth to speak, but his brother beat him to it. "This her?" he asked, staring at Shante.

Jake nodded. "Yeah . . . Shante, this is my brother, Cue."

Cue smiled. "You didn't tell me she was beautiful."

Jake and Shante gazed at each other that way, like lovebirds. Then Jake introduced me, "Cue, this is our friend Sunday."

"Sunday . . . cool name," he said.

"Thanks," I replied.

"I'm heading to the cafeteria. You people wanna join me?" he asked.

Jake and Shante said yes, but I told them, "I gotta go."

"Nice meeting you," Cue said.

"You too," I replied. "Later, Shante. Bye, Jake. Glad your mom's gonna be okay." I made a beeline out of the hospital to the bus stop.

While I waited on the bench, this man sat down beside

me. Cautiously, I looked into his face. He had a big nose and squinty eyes like Mr. Johnson. My hands started shaking, and my palms got sweaty. I got up and stood as far away as I could because I, Sunday Waters, who had never been afraid of very much, was now scared of almost everything. At night, I didn't want to close my eyes. Every loud noise made me jumpy, and if a man so much as looked at me, I wanted to run away. I watched the man closely, but when my bus finally showed up, he didn't get on. Relieved, I took a really deep breath.

On the ride home it started raining, turning the streets slick and shiny. I put my legs across the seat so no one could sit beside me, turned on my music player, and started thinking about Shante and Jake. His brother sure seemed friendly, and Jake is kind of sweet. Maybe all white boys aren't alike, I thought. Maybe I should give Jake a chance.

At the next stop, more than twenty people were waiting to get on. Some of them were fooling with their umbrellas and I was thinking, *This madness is going to take forever,* when I noticed a sign in the window of a karate school across the street. SELF-DEFENSE CLASSES FOR WOMEN AND GIRLS.

Quickly, I scribbled the telephone number and address in my notebook. And as the bus took off, I pictured myself with a black belt in karate, giving Mr. Sam Johnson a good ass kicking.

We Tight

(Shante)

"Shante, you can sit up front with Cue."

Like a gentleman, Jake opened the door and I got in. The rain had stopped, and it was still daylight as we drove through the streets toward my house. Jake had convinced me not to take the bus, but part of me wished I had. Being in the car with Cue and Jake made me feel strange, like everyone was staring at us, even though I don't think they were. Still, I felt better when we got to my block—until I saw Daddy outside trimming his hedges.

Great, I thought, here I am being dropped off by two white guys in a raggedy ride. Why did the rain have to stop? At least Daddy was facing the house and the trimmer was loud.

"Nice neighborhood," Cue commented. "Which house?"

"The gray one," I replied. As Cue slowed the car, all I could think was, Please don't let my daddy turn around before they drive away. "Thanks for the ride," I told Cue as I climbed out. "See ya, Jake."

Jake slid into the front seat and I got ready to sprint, hoping to get into the house without being seen. But before I could dash, Jake asked, "That your dad?"

He had stopped trimming the bushes and was staring at us, the hedge trimmer at his side. His mouth was open in surprise. "Yeah," I said. "Gotta go."

"I'll call you later," Jake promised.

I glanced at Daddy again. He was still gaping. "Yeah, later," I replied. As they sped away, Jake waved back at me.

Smiling sweetly, I walked toward the house. "Hi, Daddy."

Daddy didn't even look at me. Instead, his eyes followed their car. "Who were those boys, Shante?" he asked angrily.

"Jake . . . he's in my English class, and the one driving is his brother."

"Where have you been?"

"At the hospital. Their mom was in a bad car accident, so Sunday and I went there to see her after school."

"Did they bring Sunday home too?"

"No, she took the bus."

"Why didn't you take the bus with her?"

"Sunday didn't stay that long, and they offered me a ride. Is that a crime?"

"Don't get flip with me, Shante. I don't want you messed

on, 'specially by a white boy. I'm from South Carolina. You young people don't understand."

Oh, no, here we go, the "things were different in the South" sermon. "You can relax, Daddy. He's just a friend."

Daddy grumbled something under his breath, then said, "Go on in the house, little lady."

When I got to my room, the phone rang. It was Sunday. "Hey," she said.

"My daddy had a fit," I told her.

"Why?"

"Becuz he saw Jake and his brother when they dropped me off."

"And?"

"I lied and told him he's just a friend."

"Then what'd he say?"

"Go in the house."

"You think he believes you?" Sunday asked.

"I dunno, maybe," I sighed. "I really like Jake, but maybe you're right about it being too much trouble."

I waited for Sunday to say something like I told you so, but instead she said, "He seems like he's really into you. And for a white boy, Shante, he is kinda fly."

"Fly or not, you didn't see the look on my daddy's face."

"What'd you think? You know how black daddies can be 'bout their baby girls and white boys."

"I know but—"

Sunday interrupted, "But you thought it would be easy?"

"I s'poze."

"You s'pozed wrong, girly," Sunday said smugly.

"Now what?" I asked.

"I dunno. I mean if I was ever going to date a white boy, which I'm not, I'd tell anyone who had a problem with it to kiss my BA. Plus Jake introduced you to his brother."

"And after you left, I met his mother," I confided.

"Was she cool with you?"

"I guess so."

"Then how you gonna keep your blue-eyed crush on the down low?"

"So you stopped trippin', just like that?"

Sunday giggled. "Mostly. . . . We tight?"

"We tight," I replied. Having my best *girl* on my side made me feel so much better.

"You wanna take karate with me?" Sunday asked. "I'm gonna take a class to learn how to seriously kick some ass."

"Maybe," I said. "I'm really busy with my dance classes. What day?"

"I think Saturdays. I called on my way home. It's not that expensive. Plus it's worth it to be able to keep people from messin' with you."

"For real," I replied.

• • •

When I got off the phone, I began asking myself questions. Even if Sunday was okay with it, could I really deal with this thing with Jake? What if it went deep and he got into my heart? When I'm with him, it seems like there's no one else around. He's cool, sweet, and fly. But what about Daddy? And I'd almost forgotten about the Queen Bee. Once she finds out, she'll rake me over every chance she gets. As for Kyle, I knew he wouldn't have much to say, considering all the everything-but-black honeys he'd had on his arm. Still, black girls hanging out with white boys isn't that common—not like the reverse, white girls with brothers. That's so *everyday*. I imagined people with disapproving looks on their faces ogling me and Jake in public.

I flopped onto my bed, curled into a ball, and thought about Sunday's episode with the gun and now karate. Sunday had courage. I wished I did.

My cell vibrated. Jake had sent me a text message:

uronmymind.

I could almost feel Jake's hand in mine as I returned the text:

uronmine2.

I stared out the window at my daddy, who was working on the hedges right outside my room, and decided I should be honest. I yanked open the window. "Daddy!" I yelled.

He turned off the trimmer. "What's wrong, Shante?"

"Nothing."

"Then what is it?" he asked impatiently.

"That boy who dropped me off?"

"The white boy?"

"His name is Jake."

Daddy looked angry again. "What about him?"

"He's nice, and I like him. This isn't South Carolina, and you need to understand that things are changing."

There, I said it.

"I need to understand?" Daddy huffed.

I stared into his eyes like a kid begging to get off punishment. "Okay?"

"Like I told you, Shante, I don't want you gettin' messed on." But this time he left off the part about "by a white boy." "Now, shut the window so I can get back to work." He glanced at me once more before restarting his trimmer.

COLD CLEAN

(JAKE)

AFTER WE DROPPED OFF SHANTE, WE HEADED BACK TO THE hospital.

"I've been savin' my money, dude," Cue told me. "And I finally have enough for a down payment on my own place, probably a studio condo or maybe a one bedroom."

"Congrats," I said. He'd been talking about it for a long time, so I wasn't surprised. But he looked lit up like someone who'd scored the winning point in a ball game.

"So, dude, if things with the *madre* ever start to get to you, *mi casa es su casa, comprende?*"

HIV and now this accident. Poor Pretty Georgie. Both of us leaving her now didn't seem right, but I replied, "Yeah, thanks, bro."

The corridor floors in the hospital were shiny with that newly waxed look. Everything was cold and clean.

"Do you think Mom acted weird when she met Shante?" I asked Cue as we headed to her room.

"Hard to tell, dude. She is straight out of a coma."

I couldn't help but laugh.

When we got to her room, Pretty Georgie grinned at us, but then she started coughing, trying to clear her throat. "Can you go get me a chocolate milkshake, Cue?" she asked with a raspy voice.

"They have a deli down the street, that okay?"

Mom nodded.

Cue wasn't even out the door when Mom said, "Sit down, Jake, I need to talk to you."

Figuring it could only be about Shante and remembering the fight, I said, "You should get some rest."

"But I want to explain," she pleaded.

I pulled a chair up to the side of her bed. Because she'd almost died, I promised myself not to yell or anything.

"Shante's very pretty," she began. I sat still like a statue, waiting for the *but*. "And I wanted to tell you I'm sorry I said those things."

"It's okay, Mom."

"No, it isn't. It was wrong." She coughed some more, and I gave her a sip of water. There was a long pause, then she continued. "I had an African American boyfriend once."

"Really?" This was one Pretty Georgie story I'd never heard, and I thought I'd heard them all.

"Yes. In my senior year of high school. His name was Quincy, Quincy Norris. We dated for about six months."

"So what happened?"

Her eyes turned sad. "You know, parents."

"Oh. Your mom and dad didn't like it?"

"No, not my parents—his. His father was a college professor and his mom was a lawyer, and as they told me to my face, they weren't about to have their son's future ruined by a 'dalliance with a poor white girl.' Those were his mother's exact words. The next thing I knew, he'd been sent away to school. We wrote back and forth a few times, but that was that."

"Did you love him?" I asked.

Her mouth curled into a smile. "Yes, very much."

"What about your parents, didn't they care?"

"They didn't seem to mind too much. Whenever he came to the house, they were nice as could be. But after he went away, they kept telling me we wouldn't have been happy because of the way most people felt about interracial dating and marriage back then. My dad called it a recipe for trouble. And when I thought about some things that had happened when Quincy and I were together, I started to believe he was right."

"Like what kind of things?"

"Once when Quincy and I were walking down the street, holding hands, a car slowed down to a stop and this white man rolled down his window and spit at us. And another time a black woman saw us in Wal-Mart together, and when Quincy wandered off to another part of the store, she asked me, 'What's wrong, can't you find you a white boy?' I never forgot that."

"That was Minnesota and a long time ago," I told her. "Things are different now."

"I hope so." Pretty Georgie got teary eyed as she offered me her hand. I squeezed it tightly.

"I'm not a racist, Jake," she said.

A brief silence followed.

"So, about me and Shante, are you cool?" I asked.

Pretty Georgie nodded. "I'm cool."

First Date

(Mary)

"Hi, Mary," Gus said. He'd called me every night since the party, almost always talking for hours. Most people think he's shy, but he's not that way with me. And something else people don't know is that Gus is very smart.

"Call me MJ," I reminded him.

"Sorry," he said.

We were talking and joking and laughing, when suddenly he got quiet and I wondered if my phone had dropped the call. "Gus?"

"Huh?"

"Oh, I thought I'd lost the call."

"No, I'm still here," he said. More quiet.

"What's wrong?" I asked.

"Nothing."

"Liar."

Gus chuckled.

I continued my interrogation. "So what is it?"

"I was—"

I didn't give him a chance to finish. "You were what?"

"You're not making this easy," Gus replied.

"Making what easy?"

"Do you wanna go to the movies or something?" he finally blurted out.

I felt like singing. "When?"

"Saturday?"

Maybe I should have played hard to get, but I'd waited too long for this moment. "Okay, where?" I asked, hoping he couldn't tell how anxious I felt.

Gus cleared his throat. "I dunno, maybe the Century City Mall?"

"Sure . . . what time?" I knew I'd have to get permission, but I'd worry about that later.

As soon as I got off the phone with Gus, I called Ronni, but she didn't pick up. I had to tell someone. So I flipped through the *InStyle* magazine she gave me until I got to the page with the girl in the metallic bikini. "You're not going to believe this, but I have a date.

"Gus asked me if I wanted to go to the mall on Saturday. But first we're going to the hospital to visit his neighbor. That's still a date, right?"

The girl in the bikini, as always, smiled sweetly. "My first date. Plus when I got on the scale today it said one sixty-five. I lost five whole pounds. Must have been all the dancing at Ronni's party. How good is that?

"What do you think? Was it the makeup or my hair being flatironed? Fat or not, I did look pretty cute. And besides, Gus says I'm not fat, I'm plump. That sounds so much nicer.

"What do you think I should wear? Definitely flats. Or maybe tennis shoes and jeans? Not like it's the prom, right?"

I glanced in the mirror and began to have doubts. "Do you think he feels sorry for me? Or maybe it's not a real date, maybe it's a friend date. Either way, I'm going to the movies with a boy. And he's sweet. That's all that matters, right?

"Maybe high school's not a nightmare after all," I told the girl in the bikini with the perfect body, perfect hair, and perfect eyes.

I stepped outside onto the balcony right outside my room. The stars were coming out. "Oh, no, stars!" I exclaimed. The final journal entry for Ms. Hart's class. With the party and Gus and all that, I'd forgotten that it was due Friday.

Just as I began the assignment, Ronni returned my call.

"Whatsup, MJ?"

"I have a date, and it's all because of you."

She sounded surprised. "A date? With who?"

"Gus. We're going to the movies on Saturday, and if you hadn't done the makeover and invited me to your party, it never would have happened. He's really nice—"

Ronni interrupted, "MJ, can you hold on? I have another call."

"Sure."

Twenty seconds later she came back on the line. "MJ?"

"Yeah?"

"The algebra test was pretty hard," Ronni said, changing the subject.

I still wanted to talk about my date, so I assured her, "You passed. I know it," and flipped the conversation back. "Anyway we're probably going to Century City."

"Century City?"

"Me and Gus."

"Nice," she replied, then asked, "What if I didn't?"

"Didn't what?"

"Didn't pass."

"You passed, Ronni," I repeated.

She sighed, "You better be right."

"I am," I replied. "And thanks again for the makeover."

"It's nothing, *amiga*. Later."

Amiga? I thought as I hung up the phone. Ronni isn't my friend. She's only using me to get what she desperately wants—the car. Two weeks ago that would have made me feel like pigeon droppings. But things are different now.

MJ and Gus . . . I like the way that sounds.

UNTIL MIDNIGHT

(GUS)

"THANKS," I TOLD THE DRIVING SCHOOL instructor when he dropped me off outside the apartment. My first nighttime driving lesson had been easier than the ABC's. I knew I'd pass my driving test with flying colors, and I was picturing the driver's license in my hand when I bumped into Ronni as she got the mail from their box. She was wearing jeans and a black-and-white-checkered shirt, looking awesome like she always did. "Hey, Gus," she said.

"Hi, Ronni."

"I hear you and MJ have a date," she said slyly.

I smiled. "Yeah."

"You really like her?"

"She's fun."

"And very smart," Ronni added.

I agreed, "And smart."

Ronni grinned. "So call me Cupid."

"Really . . . you were trying to fix us up?" I asked.

"No, but I'll still take credit. Later." She winked, then headed upstairs.

"Bye," I said. And that was where the conversation ended.

If she had been MJ, I thought, we would have talked for hours, maybe until the sun came up, definitely until midnight. Ronni was beautiful, but with MJ I was hardly ever shy and I never felt invisible. I gazed up at Ronni's apartment and headed inside.

Late that night, the sound of a helicopter circling outside woke me. The red numbers on my digital clock read three A.M. After staying on the phone with MJ until after one, I was dead tired. I stared into the darkness, trying hard to go back to sleep, but I couldn't. So, after a while I decided to play the invisible game.

I shut my eyes tightly and imagined myself hovering like the helicopter, inside MJ's room. She was sleeping peacefully. I snuggled beside her, closed my eyes, and snoozed.

COOLICIOUS

(MARLON)

I HEARD POPS LAUGHING OUT IN THE HALL. HOW can he laugh? How can he be happy?

A knock on my door followed, and Moms came in. She flipped on the light. Pops and Chris were right behind her. I blinked a few times before I saw their smiles. "The doctor called. It's not cancer, Marlon," Moms said.

Part of me thought, *I'm dreaming.*

Pops must have read my mind. "No, you're not dreaming," he said as he pulled me to my feet and got me in a playful headlock.

"Be careful, Palmer," Moms told him.

"Shush, woman. He can handle it."

At that moment, I hooked up with a brand-new feeling, one I'd never had before—relief. In fact, I was too relieved to even be happy. I glanced over at Chris, who was standing in the doorway like a stranger. I could tell that he was really happy, and a grin cracked my face. "How you gonna stand way over there, big brother?"

Chris lurched toward me. "Baby brother," he whispered. And as we hugged, a flood of tears came pouring out of both of us.

Moms pried me from his arms and held me tightly. I felt bad for dissing her so many times since this whole thing started. "I'm sorry, Moms," I told her.

"Be quiet, Marlon," she replied.

Pops interrupted. "There is one thing."

My body stiffened. "What?" I asked.

"You do have to stay out for the whole season."

"But I can play next year?"

"Far as he can tell."

I almost didn't give a damn. Chris is right. There are more important things than basketball. Important things like living. I reached down and patted my leg. Everything was on its way to being coolicious again.

DON'T GO, MIZ HART

MS. HART ARRIVED AT HER CLASSROOM ON FRIDAY TO find a poster on the door with a big yellow happy face that said DON'T GO, MIZ HART and had been signed by everyone. She sighed. Dorian must have told them.

"Journals on the desk," she said as they entered.

Marlon was back, but still on crutches. "Even me?" he asked, waving his journal in the teacher's face.

Yesterday Dorian had informed the class that Marlon didn't have cancer and would be back on the court next season. Ms. Hart was glad. "Yes, Marlon," she replied. "Even you."

Mary scooted around him. She was still wearing her hair down, and she had on lip gloss. "Hey, Mary," Marlon said to her.

Mary rolled her eyes. "So this has made you a better person or something, right?"

Marlon's face was veiled in shame. He shrugged and took his seat.

Ronni held up what looked like a test paper and showed it to Mary. It had a big red C on it.

"I told you," Mary said, and Ronni beamed at her.

Jake entered, wearing his usual happy face. The word around school was that his mom was going to be okay. He headed to where Shante was sitting and whispered something in her ear. Shante giggled.

Sunday placed a card on Ms. Hart's desk. "Just a little sumthin' sumthin'."

"Thank you, Sunday," she told her.

"Are you really going back to New York?" Carlos asked.

"I haven't decided yet," she said carefully, wishing she hadn't said a word in the first place.

"You can't leave us, Miz Hart," Sunday pleaded.

Dorian blurted out, "Yeah, you can't."

"Don't go, Miz Hart," the class chanted.

Ms. Hart broke the mood. "Let's pick up where we left off yesterday . . . the link between poetry and music lyrics."

The clock ticked away the time as Ms. Hart taught. And the end-of-the-day bell was still ringing when Jake grabbed Shante by the hand. "Don't go, Miz Hart," Jake told her on their way out.

"Yeah, don't go, Miz Hart," Shante echoed as Jake pulled her into the hall.

"And have a good weekend," Sunday added.

Dorian darted toward the door. "Yeah . . . all that, Miz Hart."

Marlon hobbled up to her desk. "My moms told me you called twice to check up on me. . . . That was real cool of you."

"It's nothing, Marlon. I'm really glad you're okay."

"Thank you, Miz Hart. I don't want you to go either. Later."

Like most Fridays, the halls became vacant in a flash. Ms. Hart opened the card Sunday had given her. It had an angel with silver wings on the front, and inside Sunday had written, *Don't go, Miz Hart. I love you.*

Ms. Hart's eyes brimmed with tears as she gathered her students' journals together and stuffed them into her briefcase. She peeled the smiley face poster off the door, slid it under her arm, and headed to her car.

That night, Ms. Hart settled on her sofa with her cat, Purple. She picked up the remote and turned on the TV. One of the nightly entertainment shows was on. The paparazzi were all over this star and that one. Ms. Hart wondered, *How do they take it?* Fame. Hollywood. She was about to change the channel but instead flicked off the television. She grabbed her briefcase and pulled out the journals, eager to see what they'd done with the "Star on the Hollywood Walk of Fame" entries. Sunday's was on top.

SUNDAY WATERS

A STAR ON THE HOLLYWOOD WALK OF FAME

WHY DO BAD THINGS HAPPEN? I FINALLY FIGURED IT OUT. BECAUSE THEY HAVE A LOT OF STRAIGHT-UP DUMB-ASS PEOPLE ON EARTH. EVERY NOW AND THEN, I LIKE TO PRETEND THAT MY WORLD IS WONDERFUL, BUT SOMETHING ALWAYS HAPPENS TO LET ME KNOW IT ISN'T, AND FOR ALL I KNOW, IT MIGHT NEVER BE.

BUT THE PAST TWO WEEKS OF MY LIFE HAVE BEEN TOTAL MADNESS, AND I WOUND UP FEELING SCARED AS SHIT ALL THE TIME. NO WAY AM I ABOUT TO LIVE LIKE THAT, BEING AFRAID. SO I DECIDED TO TAKE KARATE. I HAVE MY FIRST CLASS ON SATURDAY. I PLAN TO GET A BLACK BELT, AND I PLAN TO BE DANGEROUS.

THE MAN WHO OWNS THE SCHOOL TOLD ME MOST PEOPLE'S MINDS ARE FULL OF NOISE, AND HE CLAIMS THAT WHEN PROBLEMS ARISE, YOU HAVE TO QUIET YOUR MIND AND FOCUS. HE TEACHES MEDITATION TOO. I SEE MYSELF GETTING INTO THAT LATER. THEN I'LL BE EVEN DEEPER THAN I ALREADY AM.

ANYWAY, AFTER I GET MY BLACK BELT, I MIGHT OPEN MY OWN SELF-DEFENSE SCHOOL. THAT'S WHAT MY ☆ ON THE HOLLYWOOD WALK OF FAME WILL BE FOR, TEACHING YOUNG LADIES TO KICK SOME BUTT AND STOP BEING AFRAID.

DORIAN GREEN

A STAR ON THE HOLLYWOOD WALK OF FAME

A MESSAGE TO MY POPS

From behind the glass wearing a jumpsuit
How you calling yourself my pops
I can't even touch you
You diss and joke
Like Comedy Club folks
But you ain't who I'm trying to be
Who I am trying to be is a pops who will
Never be incarcerated
Have a good job
Never leave my kids
Play ball with them in the street
Take them to the Grand Canyon in a huge RV
Help them with homework
Always show on parent teacher Night
They say leopards can't change
But people can
And I will
A star on the Hollywood Walk of Fame?
Give me one for that

Carlos Baraza

A Star on the Hollywood Walk of Fame

After a Santa Ana windstorm, if you hike up to the top of Griffith Park, you can see from the mountains to Catalina Island. Sometimes on a day off, I go there to stop thinking and just be. Other times I search through the shops in Little Tokyo and Chinatown. From where I live, Venice Beach is a short bus ride away. I could spend all day there. The freeways here are usually bumper-to-bumper. During a dry year, there are fires that make the air brown, and it can get hard to breathe. When it rains a lot there are landslides and people drive like maniacs. There are the rich and the homeless. So many people here want to be famous. During the daytime, it's usually noisy, but at night it quiets down.

I was born in Guatemala City, but it's not home. This is. The Big LA. And I don't want to leave.

Last week I took the bus to Hollywood Boulevard. It had been a long time since I'd been there, but nothing had really changed. The stars on the Walk of Fame, the hand- and footprints of famous people, the tourists. As I read the names on the stars, I tried hard to figure out what I could get one for. I know I won't get famous. That's okay, because I really don't want to. What I do want is to do something about immigration. I don't think it's fair to let people come here and work for ten years like my father and then turn around and tell them to go home. If someone tells me to go home, I'll say, "I am home."

Immigration reform—I'm someone who could get a star for that. Maybe even make changes. Someone needs to.

★ ★ ★ ★ ★ ★ ★

MARLON POPE

★ ★ ★

A STAR ON THE HOLLYWOOD WALK OF FAME

Ever since I was in the seventh grade, I've been a star, and believe me, people do treat you better. It feels good too, because contrary to what most people think, I was not born a gifted athlete. It took two tons of hard work to become who I am now, Marlon Pope, All-League, MVP, the three-point man.

Some people like to talk a lot about destiny, but sometimes things happen. The road you thought was going to be full of riches and fame gets a big bump in it, and everything changes.

What I learned since my surgery is that basketball's not everything, and I shouldn't put all my hope into it. Don't get me wrong; it's fine with me if I become the next superstar living large, but if I don't, that's okay too. There are definitely other things I could be good at. And now, I have a whole year to sit out and think about what those things might be.

So don't give me a star for hoops, give me a star for working hard to become who I am and for believing in myself. I mean, if I don't, who will?

★ Shante Harris ★
A Star on the Hollywood Walk of Fame

For a long time, I've been practicing posing on the red carpet, looking over my shoulder at flashing cameras, hoping to get bigger than **Beyoncé**. My last name won't even matter. I'll simply be **Shante**.

Some people say that's shallow, but when you really think about it, entertainers give something very special to us all. They get up on stage or in front of the camera and let us into their world of make-believe. People who have troubles and people who don't can escape for a while. Entertainers have been around forever. I suppose real-world drama has been getting to people from the beginning.

I want an actual star on the Hollywood Walk of Fame. It's all right to want that, isn't it? When I'm onstage, I'm different, more alive. I was born to do this. At least that's how I see it.

But I would also like to get a **Star** for standing up to my father for the first time in my life. All he ever used to talk about was the way things were in the South during segregation and he was against most white people because of it. I knew for certain he never wanted me to date someone white, so at first, I felt afraid to be out about it. But the weird thing is, once I stood up to him and told him the truth, he calmed down.

Another star I could get is for accepting that if you find love in the eyes of someone who looks different from you, it's okay because after all, love is love.

I, the one and only **Shante**, plan on getting lots of stars. These three are only the beginning. ★ ★ ★

GUS LITTLE

A STAR ON THE HOLLYWOOD WALK OF FAME

Last week, Mrs. Rosenthal, who lives upstairs from me, got sick and I had to give her CPR. Her heart had stopped, but when the paramedics came, they jolted her back to life. Right then, I decided to go to medical school to become a cardiologist.

The heart is kind of like a house. There are four rooms called chambers and valves that act like doors, opening and closing. Lately I've been wondering how the heart and love got linked. Maybe it's because they are both things we can't live without. But we can't live without lungs or a brain either. Why do we think love lives in that fist-sized house called a heart? Maybe because the heart feeds our cells and love feeds our souls? Speaking of the soul, I have two questions: where is it and what would it look like if you could see it? It's one of those mysteries, isn't it? Like how can two things look the same but be so different. Take shaving cream, for example: it looks exactly like whipped cream, but one is sweet and the other isn't even edible. It's what something is made of that's important—what's inside that counts. The same with people. Some have good hearts, and some don't. A good-hearted person can make you stop feeling shy and invisible. A good heart can work magic.

I know not all doctors deserve stars, so I asked myself what would make me one who did. The answer I came up with is that I would get a star for being a heart doctor with a heart.

Ronni Castillo

A Star on the Hollywood Walk of Fame

After high school I plan to go to beauty school to really learn hair and makeup. I've been thinking about this since the fifth grade because by then school was getting hard. Mostly I got C's except once in geography I got a B.

I also thought about maybe doing special-effects makeup, but since I started doing my own makeovers, I decided I don't want to do that.

After I finish beauty school, I'll start my own cosmetics line because, according to the lady at the makeup store where I buy most of my stuff, that's where the good money is. Then once I start to get successful, I'll hire some smart people to take care of the business part. That way I won't have to worry and I'll be able to concentrate on making new products. It's really stupid to fail if there are people to help you, right? So, I want to get a star for having a successful cosmetics company.

The only problem is that to graduate from Fairfield, I have to pass the exit exam. I never really studied too hard, but maybe if I do and keep getting tutored by my friend MJ, I can pass, because I heard it's not that hard. Maybe I'm finally getting smart after all.

Mary Holly
A Star on the Hollywood Walk of Fame

Could some genius figure out a way to make us actually want to come to high school? Who came up with this nightmare, anyway? Take all of the *teenagers* and put them in one place to see who survives. How sadistic.

It's like a human chess game, where there are only pawns, kings, and queens. The kings and queens are the stars. Pawns are lucky to get through unscathed. Pawn: from the Latin word for foot soldier. In the game of High School, I am definitely a pawn.

Until recently, I cringed when I walked through the Fairfield doors into the game. All I could think about was dropping out, acing the GED, and heading to college.

Now, however, one of the queens has taken me under her wing and given me a position as a medieval lady-in-waiting, a.k.a., a tutor. Also, another pawn has begun to court me. He is smart and sweet and definitely makes the game seem less treacherous. Consequently, my thoughts of either forfeiting or uniting the pawns and spearheading a rebellion have dissipated, at least for the time being.

As far as a star on the Hollywood Walk of Fame, who knows? The game of life is in a state of constant flux, and nobody can predict what the next move will be.

ONE NIGHT FROM ALONGSIDE THE MILKY WAY
I STOLE A TURQUOISE star
THEN QUIETLY FLOATED BACK TO EARTH
WHERE I PUT IT IN A JAR

I STILL HAVE THAT STAR, AND I KEEP IT WITH ME AT ALL TIMES. WHEN I'M LOOKING FOR A MELODY, IT INJECTS IT INTO MY SOUL. WHEN I'M SEARCHING FOR LUSH LYRICS, IT POURS THEM INTO MY SPIRIT. I MAY HAVE STOLEN THAT STAR FROM THE GALAXY, BUT IT NOW BELONGS TO ME.

THERE ARE DAYS WHEN IT BLAZES BRIGHTLY AND THE MUSIC FLOWS FREELY FROM ME. THEN THERE ARE WHAT I CALL DARK DAYS WHEN THE LIGHT FROM MY TURQUOISE STAR IS SO DIM I BEGIN TO WONDER IF IT'S A STAR AFTER ALL. NO MUSIC COMES AND DOUBT ENTERS. LIKE RIGHT NOW I'M TRYING TO WRITE A SONG ABOUT a girl WHO MAKES ME WISH I COULD GROW ANGEL'S WINGS AND CARRY HER TO THE MOON. LAST NIGHT I WONDERED WHAT IT WOULD BE LIKE TO BE ALONE WITH HER IN OUR OWN PRIVATE CRATER WAY UP THERE. BUT I CAN'T SEEM TO PUT IT INTO WORDS OR music.

THAT'S THE WAY IT IS WITH A TALENT, I'VE BEEN TOLD. AT LEAST THAT'S THE WAY IT IS WITH ME. MAYBE IT NEEDS TO REST SOMETIMES. OTHERWISE, IT MIGHT BURN ITSELF OUT. AND SO I HAVE LEARNED THAT WHEN MY STAR IS BLAZING, IT IS, AND WHEN IT'S DIM, MY STAR'S SIMPLY STORING UP ENERGY UNTIL IT blazes AGAIN.

My star will be for music.

ONE OTHER THING, WHATEVER COLOR SHELL WE WEAR,

we are all human

THAT'S ALL I HAVE TO SAY.

Ms. Hart sighed and rested the journals on her lap. She opened the card Sunday had given her and read it again.

"They're wonderful kids," she told Purple the cat. "Really good kids."

And that was when she knew. It wasn't warm winters, no snow that had led her so far from home. It was the newfound trust in Sunday's eyes, Dorian's promise to make something of his life, Marlon's budding humility, Jake's gift, Shante's bravery. It was Gus's desire to help others, gorgeous Ronni's decision to accept help with school, and wounded Mary's recovery in progress. It was Carlos's determination to stay in The Big LA, the city he calls home.

Purple nuzzled her shoulder, and Ms. Hart rubbed his head. One more year in the City of Lost Angels, she decided. At least one more year.